Laura held her breath, part of her hoping that he'd enter her bedroom...

while another, more cowardly part of her feared that was exactly what he'd do. She wasn't prepared for the stabbing disappointment she felt as his footsteps faded away.

She cracked the door just wide enough to see him enter Jamie's room. From her vantage point, she watched him touching the sleeping child with such reverence, such wonder and awe, that it raised a lump in her throat.

To see a man gaze upon her child with such tenderness cracked away the final vestige of her inner restraint. This was a prince among men, Laura decided. This was the man she'd waited for her entire life.

Then she heard Royce's footsteps descending the stairs, and she followed him as if beckoned by an invisible hand.

She didn't know what she would do, or what she would say. All she knew was that she had to be with him, and damn the consequences.

Dear Reader,

As the air begins to chill outside, curl up under a warm blanket with a mug of hot chocolate and these six fabulous Special Edition novels....

First up is bestselling author Lindsay McKenna's *A Man Alone,* part of her compelling and highly emotional MORGAN'S MERCENARIES: MAVERICK HEARTS series. Meet Captain Thane Hamilton, a wounded Marine who'd closed off his heart long ago, and Paige Black, a woman whose tender loving care may be just what the doctor ordered.

Two new miniseries are launching this month and you're not going to want to miss either one! Look for *The Rancher Next Door,* the first of rising star Susan Mallery's brand-new miniseries, LONE STAR CANYON. Not even a long-standing family feud can prevent love from happening! Also, veteran author Penny Richards pens a juicy and scandalous love story with *Sophie's Scandal,* the first of her wonderful new trilogy— RUMOR HAS IT... that two high school sweethearts are about to recapture the love they once shared....

Next, Jennifer Mikels delivers a wonderfully heartwarming romance between a runaway heiress and a local sheriff with *The Bridal Quest,* the second book in the HERE COME THE BRIDES series. And Diana Whitney brings back her popular STORK EXPRESS series. Could a *Baby of Convenience* be just the thing to bring two unlikely people together?

And last, but not least, please welcome newcomer Tori Carrington to the line. *Just Eight Months Old...* and she'd stolen the hearts of two independent bounty hunters—who just might make the perfect family!

Enjoy these delightful tales, and come back next month for more emotional stories about life, love and family!

Best,
Karen Taylor Richman
Senior Editor

Please address questions and book requests to:
Silhouette Reader Service
U.S.: 3010 Walden Ave., P.O. Box 1325, Buffalo, NY 14269
Canadian: P.O. Box 609, Fort Erie, Ont. L2A 5X3

Baby of Convenience

DIANA WHITNEY

Silhouette

SPECIAL EDITION™

Published by Silhouette Books

America's Publisher of Contemporary Romance

To Constance Martynow, a wonderful sister-in-law and devoted fan, who welcomed me into the family and has offered constant support over the years. You are deeply loved, gratefully appreciated. Thank you.

SILHOUETTE BOOKS

ISBN 0-373-24361-8

BABY OF CONVENIENCE

Copyright © 2000 by Diana Hinz

Visit Silhouette at www.eHarlequin.com

Printed in U.S.A.

Books by Diana Whitney

DIANA WHITNEY

is a three-time Romance Writers of America RITA Award finalist, *Romantic Times Magazine* Reviewers' Choice Award nominee and finalist for Colorado Romance Writers' Award of Excellence. Diana has published more than two dozen romance and suspense novels since her first Silhouette title in 1989. A popular speaker, Diana has conducted writing workshops and has published several articles on the craft of fiction writing for various trade magazines and newsletters. She is a member of Authors Guild, Novelists, Inc., Published Authors Network and Romance Writers of America. She and her husband live in rural Northern California with a beloved menagerie of furred creatures, domestic and wild. She loves to hear from readers. You can write to her c/o Silhouette Books, 300 East 42nd Street, 6th Floor, New York, NY 10017.

CANADA

N

Lake
Ontario

NEW YORK

VERMONT

Mill Creek

Syracuse

PENNSYLVANIA

MASSACHUSETTS

CONNECTICUT

New York
City

All underlined places are fictitious.

Chapter One

Bright eyes, taunting and haughty, peered from behind the gnarled trunk of a stately black oak. With an irked blink at those who so relentlessly followed, the eyes turned away, and their owner slipped into the meadow, gliding lithely through the purple profusion of wild lupine toward the one place no one dared to follow.

"Maggie, don't be a tease." A croak of desperation broke the command into a whining supplication. "Don't hide from us, precious, we only want to help. You know how much we love you."

Unmoved by the poignant plea, Maggie ducked into a neatly trimmed hedgerow at the far side of the meadow, and disappeared.

"Me firsty."

"Shh, sweetums, I know you're thirsty." Laura Michaels shifted the baby in her arms, wiped a smudge of tree sap from his wind-chafed cheek. As she peeked through the pruned thicket, her heart sank at the expanse of manicured lawns and lush, formal garden leading up to an architectural marvel that could only be described as a mansion. "We have to be real quiet for a few minutes, okay? Then we can go home, and Mama will get you a big glass of juice."

Jamie rubbed his eyes, popped a thumb in his mouth and laid his head on his mother's shoulder as she carefully eased through the shrubbery, ever watchful lest her presence on these hallowed grounds be detected. Rich people lived here. Rather, one rich person in particular.

Laura had never met Royce Burton. She hadn't even seen him beyond an across-the-street glimpse of tailored cashmere as he'd whisked from the corporate office of Burton Technologies into a gleaming Mercedes with tinted windows. Everyone in Mill Creek knew about Burton, the elusive entrepreneur who'd created an industrial complex that had turned an area in upstate New York on the brink of financial ruin into a thriving boomtown. Mill Creek citizens worshiped him. Not surprising, since he signed the majority of their paychecks.

Laura remained cynical, although she hadn't been immune to the monetary temptation that had seduced most of her friends and neighbors. She also coveted a job at Burton Technologies. Desperate means for desperate measures, she supposed, although she understood people like Royce Burton all too well. Experience had taught her that wealthy folks were a breed unto themselves. Contemptuous, self-indulgent. Cruel.

Maggie couldn't have chosen a worse spot to isolate

herself from the world. Laura could not have been more determined to rescue her beloved Maggie from making a horrific mistake in judgment. "Hold on, sweetums," she murmured to the fussing baby in her arms. "Just a few more minutes, okay?"

A flash of movement caught Laura's eye. A blooming daylily at the south wing of the huge home rustled. She gave another wary glance around the lush grounds. Then, cradling her sleepy child in her arms, she crept forward.

Ducking beneath a cantilevered bay window, she slipped to the rear of the house just in time to see the final vibration of foliage in front of an open basement window.

"Oh, criminey." So much for the hope that Maggie had found refuge in a separate toolshed, or some other structure from which she could be quietly extricated without disturbing the mansion's owner.

She swallowed hard. "Hold on to your diapers, Jamie. Looks like we're about to have ourselves an up-close-and-personal introduction to the richest, most powerful and most frightening man in the entire town."

The woman's eyes were ice blue, cool to the point of frigid. Strands of gray muted the reddish hue of hair faded by time and twisted into a bun as tight as her jawline.

She eyed Laura, her gaze lingering on the squirming child long enough to reflect a hint of disdain. "Is Mr. Burton expecting you?"

"No." Shifting as Jamie gave a sideways lurch, Laura tightened her grip on her fidgeting son and struggled to maintain her composure. She'd met women like this before. Too many of them, actually. Household terrors who ruled the inner workings of their employer's homes as if they'd been blessed by royal decree. "It's urgent that I speak with him at once."

"Impossible. Mr. Burton is in conference."

"But it's Sunday." Desperate, Laura turned her attention toward a masculine voice filtering from somewhere beyond the gleaming marble foyer. "I won't take much of his time."

Unmoved, the woman, who appeared to be in her midfifties, squared her shoulders, took a sideways step as she prepared to close the massive carved door. "I suggest you call his office in the morning. His personal assistant will either set up an appointment—" cool blue eyes once again settled on the baby in Laura's arms "—or refer you to his personal attorney."

Shocked by the implication, Laura bristled. "Mr. Burton must have quite a morals deficit for you to presume every visiting child is the issue of a tawdry affair."

The moment the angry words rumbled off her tongue, she regretted them. An unrestrained temper was not usually one of Laura's flaws, except where her son was concerned. An insult to Jamie was intolerable, even if it meant alienating her only means of locating the elusive Mr. Burton—and the even more elusive Maggie.

"How dare the likes of you insult a man of Mr. Burton's impeccable standards?" A crimson flush stained the furious woman's crepey throat, and a flash of embarrassed fury narrowed her eyes. Had it not been for the fortuitous diversion of a booming masculine voice, Laura had no doubt the massive doors would have been instantly slammed in her face.

"Marta!"

The distracted woman spun around, gazing like an anxious lapdog in the direction from which brusque footsteps echoed. "Get Robinson at the Brussels office on the line. Also, call Dave Henderson. Have him call a finance committee meeting for this afternoon."

Taking advantage of the tight-jawed door sentry's inattention, Laura decided it was now or never. Tucking Jamie tightly against her shoulder, she stepped inside before the startled Marta could stop her.

A blur of movement caught Laura's eye as a dark-haired man in a tailored suit strode out of a room where a magnificent wall lined with leather-bound books was visible through an arched doorway.

He moved with purpose and determination, although his gaze was riveted on a sheaf of documents he held in one hand. A cellular phone was clasped in the other. "Tell Henderson to bring the updated revenue projections and cash-flow statements, along with the revised production estimates—"

He glanced up, did a double take when he saw Laura. He didn't jerk to a stop, exactly. Rather, he slowed with a fluid grace, a man whose every movement was clearly practiced and precise.

A questioning glance at the older woman was met with an apologetic tone that was a striking contrast to the haughty demeanor she'd displayed a moment earlier. "I'm terribly sorry, Mr. Burton, I tried to tell this...woman...that you weren't receiving—"

Laura interrupted. "I'm sorry to disturb you, Mr. Burton, but it's urgent that I speak with you immediately."

He hiked an eyebrow, allowed his gaze to slip unobtrusively along the length of her body before settling with unnerving intensity on her face. "And who might you be?"

She moistened her lips, oddly intimidated. He was only a man, after all, albeit a man whose mere presence filled a room, demanding immediate recognition. "My name is Laura Michaels."

Marta stepped forward, hands clasped tightly enough to whiten her veined knuckles. "Shall I call Security?"

"Not at the moment." There was no trace of a smile on Royce's surprisingly youthful face, no hint of humor in his eyes. He slipped the cell phone into his coat pocket, tucked the sheaf of documents under his arm. "Ms. Michaels has one minute to convey this matter of urgency."

Jamie squirmed in Laura's arms, extracting his thumb with a pitiful whine. "Firsty, Mama."

"Shh, I know you are, sweetie. Just a few more minutes."

Royce regarded the child without visible emotion, although his eyes appeared to warm for a moment. A very brief moment. "You have fifty-five seconds remaining, Ms. Michaels. I suggest you make the most of them."

Taking a deep breath, Laura filled her lungs, emptied them slowly and managed to meet his unwavering stare without trembling. "I have reason to believe that your basement is being occupied without your knowledge or consent."

Whatever he'd expected to hear, that clearly was not it. A muscle twitched along a jaw that was firmer and stronger than Laura had expected. No other expression of surprise was allowed, although she noticed him blink twice, a revealing gesture she doubted he meant to display. "On what do you base that interesting speculation?"

"I followed her here."

"I see."

Laura was fascinated by the practiced ease with which he conducted himself. Every muscle in his face impassive, his eyes carefully steadied to reveal nothing beyond that which he wished to reveal. There was no twist of fingers, no absentminded straightening of cuffs or brushing of invisible lint. This was a man used to being in control, in control of himself, of others, and of any situation, no matter how unexpected or startling.

Laura moistened her lips. "I believe she entered through the basement window."

Still no change in expression, no gleam of interest in eyes so dark a woman could get lost in them. "Is this individual a fugitive of some kind?"

Feeling profoundly silly all of a sudden, Laura was annoyed by an irksome dryness in her mouth. "I wouldn't exactly call her a fugitive."

"So we are in no danger?"

She allowed herself the luxury of a smile. "That rather depends, I suppose—"

He glanced at his watch. "Your minute is up, Ms. Michaels. Thank you for the information. We'll certainly look into the matter."

At the signal, the annoying Marta person spun to grasp Laura's elbow, no doubt preparing to shuffle her out the door. "No, wait, you don't understand." Wriggling out of the older woman's grasp, Laura blurted, "There's more."

Again he hiked that well-formed brow in what Laura decided was a deliberate gesture designed to demean those toward whom it was so purposefully aimed. "I've assured you that the matter will be investigated."

Ego trips by powerful men brought out the devil in Laura. She could have simply told him what he needed to know, but she found that damnable arched eyebrow irksome.

Lifting her chin, she narrowed her eyes, cooled her voice. "If you choose to investigate without my presence, Mr. Burton, I can assure you that your question of Maggie's ability to do harm will be answered in a manner that will definitely not be to your liking."

He studied her with the bold, unblinking stare that strong men use against those who would challenge them. When he spoke, however, his voice had softened in tone, if not in authority. "Marta, continue arrangements for the finance committee meeting as I requested. You may hold off placing the Brussels call until I return."

Marta was clearly flabbergasted. "Return from where?"

"Why, from escorting Ms. Michaels to the basement." He laid the documents on a nearby sideboard before cupping Laura's elbow with a gentleness that was surprising and guiding her to an enameled doorway in the base of a curving staircase off the foyer.

"Actually," he whispered when out of the frantic Marta's hearing range, "we wealthy elitists prefer to call it a wine cellar. That sounds much more privileged, don't you agree?"

An embarrassed heat slithered up Laura's throat at the realization that her disdain for his lifestyle had been so obvious. Royce Burton was apparently a man who let little slip by his perception.

Still, there was no excuse for rudeness. She regretted

her own pomposity in daring to judge him for the sin of having more than he needed while others never had enough.

She cleared her throat. "I apologize if I've offended you, Mr. Burton."

The vaguest trace of amusement softened his reply. "I'm not easily offended, Ms. Michaels, although you are certainly welcome to make the attempt."

As he opened the cellar door, she chanced a glance upward. That's when she saw it, the upward tilt of sculpted lips, the soft gleam transforming ordinary brown eyes into glowing amber. He was smiling.

The effect was devastating. *Oh, Maggie,* she thought as her heart gave a palpable thump of longing. *What have you gotten us into this time?*

Soft lights lined the cellar, illuminating rich oak wine racks filled with dusty bottles, presumably containing the most extravagant and rarest of vintages. A split-oak tasting table posed in the center of the room, upon which a silver corkscrew and several pieces of crystal stemware had been placed. Wooden crates were stacked in a corner. Thin curls of straw packing material were strewn over the hardwood floor, and at the apex of the cinder-block wall a thin slice of daylight sprayed from the narrow opening beneath a basement window that had been painted black.

Beside her, Royce glanced around with mild curiosity. "Everything seems to be in order."

"Not everything," Laura murmured. Her gaze was riveted on a pair of golden eyes gleaming in a pool of shadow beyond one of the massive wine racks. Tightening her grasp on her weary son, she glided forward, murmuring softly. "So there you are, precious. Shame on you for worrying me half to death."

The golden eyes blinked.

Laura felt Royce move behind her. "What on earth…?" A warning hiss moved him back a step. He straightened, his practiced impassivity melting into obvious astonishment. "My God."

"Don't frighten her," Laura said. "She's not fond of strangers."

On cue, Maggie issued a low growl, then turned with a swish and slunk into the shadowy corner.

Moving quietly, Laura followed, knelt down and saw what she had feared. There was her beloved Maggie, nested in an empty wine crate softened with supple straw packing, settling down to nurse her brood of newborn kittens. "Oh, dear," Laura murmured. "Five of them. I never counted on so many."

Jamie suddenly yanked his thumb out of his mouth, squealing with delight. "Kitty, kitty!" He lurched forward, fat arms outstretched toward his beloved pet.

Laura reeled him back a moment before he squirted out of her grasp. "No, no, honey, Maggie doesn't want to be petted right now. She's feeding her babies."

"Babies?" Royce's voice changed from quizzical to horrified in the space of a heartbeat. *"Babies?"*

A pleasant warmth on her back confirmed that he'd ventured forth to observe for himself.

"It is a cat," he said finally.

Laura smiled. "Indeed."

"I detest cats."

Her smile faded. "I'm sorry to hear that."

A draft chilled her spine as he stepped aside, perhaps for a better view of the feline family, perhaps simply to put an extra foot of distance between them. "This is totally unacceptable."

Heaving a sad sigh, Laura struggled to contain the gleeful toddler while hoisting herself to her feet. "I was afraid that it would be."

"How could this happen?" he demanded.

"Well, Maggie is a girl cat, you see, and she met this perfectly charming boy cat, whereupon they did what little girl cats and little boy cats have been doing for ever so long—"

"Very amusing." That same traitorous muscle twitched along his jaw. "I'm familiar with the biological process of feline reproduction. What bewilders me is the process by which this particular feline chose to complete the process—" his voice rose, startling Jamie "—*in my basement.*"

"Wine cellar," Laura corrected him, then turned her attention to comforting her son, whose lip was quivering. "There, there, sweetie, it's okay." Tears gleamed in the baby's wide brown eyes. He hiccuped, gulped and emitted a thin wail of distress. Laura hugged him, coaxed a damp strand of sable hair from his moist baby forehead. "Shh, Mama is here, everything is all right."

Royce frowned. "Is the child ill?"

"No. Loud voices frighten him."

Clearly stunned, Royce rocked back a step, regarding the trembling toddler with unabashed shock. "I caused the child's distress?"

"Not deliberately, of course. Jamie just..." She allowed the words to dissipate, unwilling to divulge details of the experiences that had led her beloved child to quake with fear at the sound of a booming male voice.

"I'm so sorry."

Genuine remorse cracked his dispassionate demeanor, a tiny flaw of humanity that surprised her.

Before she could study it more intently, he rearranged his features, focused on the baby and spoke with exaggerated gentleness. "Please forgive me, young man. It was not my intention to upset you."

A moist streak stained the child's pink cheek. Jamie eyed the impeccably groomed stranger who had paused several feet away as if fearing to step any closer. "Me firsty," the toddler whined.

"Are you now? That is something we can certainly rectify." With that tantalizing hint of a smile, Royce strode to a wall by the curving wrought-iron staircase and flipped an intercom switch.

A moment later, a taut, familiar female voice replied. "Yes, Mr. Burton?"

"Marta, please bring a pitcher of orange juice to the cellar."

"Orange juice?" came the bewildered reply.

"Hold on a moment." He glanced at Laura. "Would you or the child prefer something else? I can offer an assortment of fruit juices. Also, coffee, iced tea, your choice of carbonated beverage or wine, if you'd like."

"No, thank you. Orange juice would be lovely."

"Something to eat, perhaps? Is the child hungry?"

"That's kind of you, but it's nearly his lunchtime. A snack would spoil his appetite."

"Very well." He turned back toward the intercom. "That will be all, Marta. Thank you."

After clicking off the speaker switch, Royce pursed his lips thoughtfully, casting first a quick look at Laura and Jamie, then glancing over his shoulder to the cozy nest where a purring, contented Maggie was in the process of bathing a mewing ball of orange-and-white fluff.

Laura followed his gaze. "My best guess is that the kittens are about one week old. Maggie disappeared for several days, and when she finally returned, it was obvious that she was no longer pregnant. I've been following her for days to find her birthing nest."

"I see." He studied the mother cat's methodical grooming of her brood for a moment. "I'm certainly no expert on feline behavior, but I was under the impression that most animals chose a location in which they feel safe and comfortable for such an, er, auspicious event."

"Yes, well, I'm afraid poor Maggie feels neither safe nor comfortable in our temporary living quarters. You see, we had to... I mean, we chose to move from an apartment in the downtown district to share a mobile home with a friend."

Chose to move. A clever euphemism for eviction, which didn't escape the astute Royce Burton's notice if the knowing gleam in his eye was any clue.

"At any rate, the accommodations are rather cramped, and my friend has two older children who didn't mean to torment Maggie, although she understandably had little tolerance for them, given her delicate condition."

He nodded politely. "These temporary living quarters, might they be included in the mobile home park to the south of the grounds?"

Presuming he was referring to his own expansive property when he used the word *grounds,* Laura nodded. "It's just temporary," she repeated lamely. "Until we can find something that suits our needs."

Something that was basically free, since she was currently unemployed. She'd had the audacity to slap the roving hand of her supervisor, and had been summarily dismissed from her job as a discount store clerk. At the time she'd worn her termination as a badge of honor. Now she saw it only as having sawed off her own breathing appendage. It wasn't as if she had the luxury of pride now. She had a child to consider, a child whose mother was unemployed and teetering on the brink of bankruptcy.

Royce regarded her. "Sharing such modest living accommodations with another family must be difficult for you and your husband."

"I'm divorced." Laura's reply was issued with more firmness than intended.

Instantly Royce's eyes cooled in disapproval. "I see. And your friend, is he also divorced?"

"As a matter of fact, *she*—" Laura stressed the gender-specific pronoun and was satisfied by his guilty cringe "—is happily married, although her husband is on a temporary work assignment out of town."

He issued a curt, apologetic nod. "Forgive the errant presumption."

"As I said, the living arrangements are purely temporary. Unfortunately, there is hardly enough room for the people, let alone six animals."

"May I presume that you are financially unable to secure alternative living quarters?"

That was an understatement. "The truth is that even if I found a job tomorrow it would be months before I could save up enough money to make a deposit on a larger place."

Laura couldn't fathom why she was telling him this, but the words nonetheless streamed out as if this powerful and put-upon individual was actually interested in the life story of a virtual stranger.

A thin laugh slipped from her lips, high-pitched and embarrassingly desperate. "I know this isn't your problem. You can't possibly care about my little trials and tribulations. It's just that I honestly don't know what I'm going to do about Maggie and her babies."

"Aren't there shelters for this kind of occurrence?"

Laura was horrified. "I could never put Maggie's babies in an animal shelter."

"Why not? That's what they are there for."

"They are there to take pets that nobody wants, and if they can't find homes for them, to put them humanely out of their misery."

From the corner of her eye she saw Royce stiffen, and was relieved to note that he didn't detest cats enough to be immune to the horror of euthanizing healthy animals because nobody wants them.

Laura pressed her advantage. "There's no way to find good homes for the kittens until they're old enough to leave their mother. I mean, their little eyes aren't even open yet." She paused, swallowed hard. "Meanwhile, I clearly have a bit of a problem."

"Clearly," Royce agreed.

As Laura was mentally formulating what to say next, Marta descended the stairs carrying a frosty crystal pitcher of orange juice.

Obviously unhappy, the woman thumped the pitcher on the table, then glanced toward the corner and spotted the feline family. "Oh, Mother of God!" she shrieked. "What are those creatures doing here?"

Royce favored her with a bland stare. "At the moment, they are having lunch."

"Box them up at once," Marta sputtered. "Get them

out of here before their hairy filth spreads into the rest of the house.''

"Oh, I don't think that will be much of a problem," Royce said pleasantly. "The animals will be confined to the cellar. Ms. Michaels will, of course, be allowed access at any time she deems necessary to feed them and care for their needs."

It took a moment for Laura to decipher the significance of what had just been said.

Marta, however, reacted instantaneously. "It's unconscionable to permit these vile creatures to remain inside your living quarters. They may be diseased, infested with parasites. It's an abomination."

"I suspect we'll manage to muddle through this crisis without creating a global plague." Royce stepped to the oak tasting table and poured two glasses of juice, handing one to Jamie, who snatched it with such excited haste that the sticky liquid sloshed on Laura's clothing.

"What of my duties?" Marta asked. "I cannot perform my work efficiently if I am constantly interrupted."

A covert glance confirmed the older woman's obvious revulsion as juice ran down the toddler's chin to soak into his tiny striped T-shirt. Obviously this was not a woman who tolerated untidiness in any form.

Royce didn't seem particularly perturbed either by the messy process of quenching a toddler's thirst or the potential interruption in Marta's duties. "Then I suggest," he told her mildly, "that you supply Ms. Michaels with a key so she may come and go without disturbing you."

Marta went absolutely white. "You can't be serious."

He gave her a quiet look that rocked her back a step. "Have you known me to joke?"

Deflated, the woman merely shook her head.

"Excellent." He turned to Laura, regarding her with a casual dispassion that didn't quite match the probing intensity of his eyes. "I trust the arrangements meet your approval, Ms. Michaels?"

It took a moment to locate her voice, a moment during which Laura steadied the toddler's grasp as he greedily gulped his juice. "Your offer is exceptionally generous," she said finally. "I'm deeply grateful."

"Then it's settled." With a brusque nod, he spun on his heel, ascended the curving stairs and disappeared with the incensed Marta right on his heels.

Laura could hardly believe her good fortune. A man who supposedly abhorred cats had just offered her not only the unfettered use of his wine cellar as a feline nursery, but was also allowing her free access to provide the care Maggie and her kittens would require.

Spirits soaring, Laura was convinced that the spate of bad luck that had so relentlessly plagued her was finally at an end.

In truth, it was just beginning.

The group of tailored financiers gathered in the leather-bound study, droning on about cash-flow projections and capital investment forecasts.

Royce tried to concentrate on the figures. Decisions made here would affect lives, thousands of lives.

Despite outward success, the market share of Burton Technologies was slipping. Research and development was stagnant. They desperately needed an infusion of cash. Investment capital. Lots of it.

This was a business discussion of tremendous importance. And all he could think about was the color of Laura Michaels's eyes.

They were green. Not loden, not olive, not even the hue of warm grass in springtime. Rather, they were a multihued tapestry of every verdant tint and tone that nature could supply.

In the bright foyer light they had seemed almost transparent, the pale shade of cymbidium orchid leaves brightened with sparkling emerald. In the amber illumination of the cellar, they'd taken on the golden glow of a summer pond at sunset.

More than the color of those haunting eyes, Royce had been affected by their clarity. The lush young woman with the haunting smile had hidden nothing, exposed all.

He was fairly certain she was unaware that her emotions were so blatantly revealed. He also doubted she realized that her habit of scraping her lower lip with her teeth while trying to construct an evasively truthful reply was quite revealing to a man who'd created a career out discerning information that others wished to hide.

The child was interesting, too. Obviously well-loved and carefully nurtured, judging by his bright-eyed curiosity. Dark eyes, too. Deep brown, coffee-colored, closer to Royce's own eye color than to that of his mother's.

The boy's fear of loud voices was telling as well. He wondered about it, didn't care for the speculation crowding his thoughts. His own father had been a controlled man, neither outgoing nor withdrawn. He'd been brilliant, of course. Royce had loved him, admired him, had been desperate to please him.

He'd never succeeded in pleasing him, but might

have done so eventually if he hadn't died so young, leaving Royce's mother to work herself into an early grave trying to support herself and her son. Having found himself alone at a relatively early age, he'd learned to rely on self-approval for motivation.

For the most part that had been enough.

A familiar voice broke into his thoughts. "What is that abominable sound?" Dave Henderson was asking. "You'd better have a service call on the air-conditioning, Royce. It sounds as if one of the unit bearings has blown."

Blinking, Royce considered the sound in question, a series of thin squeaks emanating from the air ducts.

Mewing kittens, he decided, and was besieged by fresh annoyance at the intrusion.

He couldn't fathom why he'd allowed the irksome animals to stay. It was foolish, and Royce Burton was not a man who accepted foolishness, not even from himself.

"The presentation needs work," Royce announced, anxious to redirect attention back to the problem at hand. "You've shown how the infusion of investment capital will assist our expansion efforts without offering a reciprocal incentive."

Henderson blinked, swallowed, touched his tie. "I know. That's rather a problem, since there doesn't appear to be any. We need them. They don't need us."

Royce understood that Henderson was referring to the Belgian directors of Marchandt Limited, the most prestigious investment firm in Europe. "Then we'll have to develop a reason for them to need us."

"There is one option...." Henderson's voice trailed off as he feigned flipping through a thick document, spiral-bound and bristling with sticky yellow notes.

"We could, ah, offer to transfer our research and development division to Brussels. Economic incentive to their personal turf, so to speak."

The suggestion came as no surprise to Royce. He doubted any of his staff could conceive of an option he hadn't already considered, and discarded. "We'd lose thousands of local jobs."

"An unfortunate side effect," Henderson agreed.

Steepling his fingers, Royce spoke quietly. "Mill Creek is a small town. An economic blow like that could destroy its economy."

"There would be a significant economic effect, to be sure. However, Mill Creek existed before Burton Technologies chose it to be the homesite, and would still exist if we moved the entire complex somewhere else." Henderson sighed, rubbed his forehead. "Hell, I don't like the idea, either, but if there's any other option I haven't thought of it."

Neither had Royce. "Then keep thinking."

"But—"

"That option is unacceptable. Come up with another." Royce stood. Six stiff-suited executives lurched to their feet in unison. "We have six weeks before the Marchandt directors arrive. I expect all the loose ends to be tied up before then and a suitable quid pro quo available for negotiation. Marta will show you out."

With that, the executives filed out of the study, talking quietly among themselves. Only Henderson stayed behind, which wasn't unusual since he was a trusted friend as well as Royce's right-hand man.

"About those loose ends," Dave said as Royce poured aged Scotch into a pair of cut-crystal glasses. "There's something I've been meaning to discuss with you."

Royce handed his friend one glass, took a sip from his own and studied a thin line of moisture forming across his finance director's upper lip.

Dave took a healthy gulp, wheezed, coughed, then twirled the glass between his palms. "You know, Europeans are not always a liberal bunch, particularly when it comes to business. They have strictly conservative views about money, and about—" he sucked a breath, took another swallow "—family."

Royce waited.

Dave cleared his throat. "Marchandt himself is Old World, comes from generations of wealth and power. He can list his ancestors back to the time of the Crusades. He inherited the company from his father, as did his father before him, and already has his sons in the business ready to carry on the family tradition." Puffing his cheeks, he blew out a breath, meeting Royce's gaze directly. "Do you remember that magazine article that came out a while back?"

"That silly 'Bachelor of the Year' thing in *Finance and World Reports*?" Royce snorted. He remembered the article well. He had fired the marketing executive who'd insisted he give the interview in the first place. "Idiotic piece of tabloid trash. I canceled my subscription in protest."

"Yes, well, to you it's tabloid trash, to Western Europe it's considered the pinnacle of financial trade information. When I went to Brussels last month, Marchandt himself had a copy of that issue on the corner of his desk."

That got Royce's attention. He leaned forward, ignored the telltale jitter of a muscle stress-twitching just below his ear. "You're just getting around to mentioning this to me?"

Dave shrugged. "I'd already handled the situation."

"How?"

"I told him the article was basically a publicity stunt by a rogue marketing executive who was no longer employed by our firm."

"Good."

"I told him there was nothing to the allegations of wild parties, beautiful starlets on each arm and the speculation that you were the real father of Madonna's love child."

"Good."

"I told him you were committed to your, er, family."

Royce narrowed his gaze. "I don't have a family."

"Well, boss, you've got six weeks to hunt one up. I told him you were a doting husband and father." Dave drained his glass, set it on a polished mahogany desk by the study window and heaved the long-suffering sigh of a man ascending a gallows. "Am I fired?"

"No." Setting his own glass aside, Royce brushed his palms lightly and pushed away from the plush burgundy recliner against which his hip had been propped. "The formality of employment termination isn't required for a dead man."

Dave paled visibly.

Muttering, Royce spun away. There were cats in the cellar. The company was going to hell in a European handbasket. His entire life was in chaos.

And all he could think about was the color of Laura Michaels's eyes.

Chapter Two

"Oh, my God. Not again." The slamming screen door shook the mobile home to its foundation. Wendy Wyatt stomped inside, her furious gaze riveted on the legal documents in Laura's hand. "What is it this time, another harassment suit claiming you've ruined the family name by divorcing that rotten, good-for-nothing son of theirs? A demand for punitive damages because their grandchild once puked on an heirloom quilt? A request to return the antique wedding ring you had to hock to pay the attorney fees for their last round of lawsuits?"

A response would be pointless, since Laura knew her dear friend wouldn't stop venting long enough to listen, anyway. She simply handed over the document in question, crossed into the cramped kitchen and poured herself a glass of water while Wendy read the newest Summons and Complaint, which had been presented to

Laura upon her return from Royce Burton's extravagant home.

Behind her, paper crinkled. Her roommate issued a stunned gasp. "That's impossible. How can your ex-laws demand full custody of your son? I mean, that sort of thing just doesn't happen…does it?"

It took Laura a moment to steady trembling hands and mop up the water she'd spilled on the counter. With a deep breath, a feigned calm, she faced Wendy with what she hoped was a poised and thoughtful expression. "Apparently it does happen, according to that duly recorded hunk of mumbo jumbo."

Wendy's face crumpled as if tears were imminent. "How can they do this? I mean, first that lying piece of dog drool they sired humiliates you by humping every female that crosses his line of sight, then when you finally divorce the obnoxious cur, he signs over his assets to his parents and runs off to Europe to avoid paying child support for his own kid. What kind of people are these, anyway?"

"Rich people." Heaving a sigh, Laura wiped the wet counter, tossed the dishrag over the faucet and swallowed a surge of anger so bitter it nearly choked her. "Money talks. If you have enough of it, ethics don't matter. You can buy your own morality."

This was the third lawsuit the Michaelses had filed against Laura since she'd had the audacity to leave their son, a spoiled young man whose once-endearing boyish alacrity soon disintegrated into adolescent immaturity, and whose taste for extravagance was legend despite the pesky fact that he'd never worked a day in his life.

The Michaelses' first lawsuit had demanded a visitation schedule so onerous it would have required

Laura to spend thousands of dollars a year shuttling Jamie hundreds of miles back and forth to his grandparents' Connecticut home, and would have resulted in the baby spending more time with his grandparents than with his own mother.

When the court awarded only minimal visitation and required the Michaelses to pay transportation costs, their desire to see their grandson dissipated. They'd never made the visitation arrangements and hadn't seen Jamie since he was an infant. He was now twenty-six months old.

The next lawsuit had demanded punitive damages, maintaining that the divorce had supposedly damaged her ex-husband's psyche so badly that he'd been forced to leave the country to heal his broken heart, thereby depriving his parents of his companionship. Fortunately, the court pointed out that since the senior Michaelses were financing their son's European lifestyle, they could avail themselves of his companionship by simply cutting off his living allowance. Laura had thought that would be the end of the legal harassment.

She'd obviously underestimated them. Again.

"Why are they doing this?" Wendy whispered.

Biting her lip, Laura stared into the stack of sticky cereal bowls and used juice glasses. Panic was a mortal enemy, one she'd fought most of her life. This time, it was winning.

"They've learned that I lost my job," she whispered. "The custody petition claims I'm financially unable to care for my son." The dirty dishes blurred beneath a film of tears. "They might win this one, Wendy. I don't know what I'd do if I lost Jamie. I just don't know what I'd do...."

"Oh, hon." Tossing the legal papers on a sofa cluttered with toy cars and comic books, Wendy rushed into the kitchen, wrapped Laura in a fierce hug. "I wish there was something I could do. My supervisor would hire you in a heartbeat if there was an opening." Wendy, like so many residents of Mill Creek, worked for Burton Technologies. "The only positions available are professional or scientific, requiring university degrees and extensive experience."

That came as no news to Laura, who'd been pounding the pavement all over town. "Don't worry about me. I'll find something." Stifling a sniff, Laura forced a brave smile and a cheery tone. "I've got an appointment tomorrow morning with the assistant manager of Quick 'n' Good Food Mart. They need cashiers for the night shift."

"Night shift?"

"Yes, that would be perfect, wouldn't it? Since I'd be home during the day, you wouldn't have to pay for after-school care for Tim and Danny."

"Uh-huh." Wendy narrowed her gaze. "And you plan to sleep...when?"

"Whenever." Issuing a laugh that sounded only slightly maniacal, Laura returned to washing dishes with an almost desperate vengeance. "The most important thing right now is providing emotional and financial security for my son. One way or the other, that's exactly what I'm going to do."

"Of course it is." Wendy retrieved a dripping glass from the dish drainer and spoke as she dried it. "The Michaelses won't win this, Laura. Your lawyer will have this thing thrown out of court before you can blink twice."

A tremor shifted from shoulder to spine, tightening Laura's stomach and nearly buckling her knees. She was thirty-one-years old, and her life was in shambles. "I don't have a lawyer anymore. He's suing me, too."

Wendy stiffened, set the glass aside with cautious deliberation. "What?"

Avoiding her friend's incredulous stare, Laura turned away, busying herself by piling breakfast dishes in the sink. Only when she felt Wendy's fingers curl into the flesh of her upper arm did she offer further explanation. "I haven't been able to make payments on his bill." She turned on the faucet and blasted a squirt of liquid detergent into an explosion of white foam. "He's turned me over to a collection agency."

The pressure on Laura's arm eased as Wendy released her grip and exhaled all at once, issuing a peculiar hiss that lifted the fine hairs on the back of Laura's neck. Her skin cooled as her roommate turned away. "Why didn't you tell me?"

"You have your own problems." Grabbing a bowl, Laura washed it, rinsed it and set it into the drainer without so much as a second glance. "And I'm one of them."

"You're not a problem. You know I love having you here."

Laura smiled over her shoulder. "You're such a sweet liar."

With a sheepish shrug and a twinkle of humor, Wendy dragged a dish towel from the door handle of the refrigerator. "All right, all right, so a friend in need is a damned nuisance—"

"Mom!" The screen door blasted open, and a tow-headed nine-year-old screeched into the small living room, nearly knocking over the rickety knickknack table that held a small television set. "Danny's hogging the bike! It's my turn to ride it, and he won't let me."

"Work it out," Wendy muttered. "You know the rules."

"But it's my turn!" The boy's wail of frustration was joined by a cranky cry from the rear of the mobile home.

Exasperated, Wendy jammed her hands on her hips, scowling at her eldest son. "You woke up the baby."

"That's all right," Laura said, wiping her hands on a tea towel. "Nap time is almost over, anyway." Actually, she'd hoped Jamie would sleep for at least another half hour, but realized such luxury was a futile dream in a chaotically crowded environment where quiet was a precious commodity and privacy was nonexistent.

As she hurried through the small living room to one of the two diminutive bedrooms at the rear of the mobile home, Laura tuned out the sounds of scolding and wailing behind her to focus on the cries of her waking baby.

She slipped into the darkened room from which the two young Wyatt boys had been evicted. Knowing that Wendy's children had been relegated to the sofa only increased Laura's guilt at the terrible imposition her presence imposed on her friend.

"There, there," she crooned, ducking her head to sit on the lower bunk where Jamie sobbed pitifully. The upper bunk was where Laura slept. "Mama's here, sweet boy." She gathered the baby in her arms, smoothing his damp hair, kissing his moist little cheek. "Mama will always be here, my precious. Always."

One way or another, it was a promise she was determined to keep.

Royce glanced up as Henderson rubbed his eyelids with the heels of his hands, and stifled a yawn. "Big night?''

"Yeah." Henderson stretched, then scooped the an-
notated draft contract from the edge of the expansive
mahogany desk in Royce's home study. "My daughter
didn't get home from her date until 2:00 a.m., my wife
screamed at her until 3:00 a.m., the baby is teething,
and I've been popping antacids since dawn."

"I see. And this is the life of married bliss you've
been nagging me to emulate?"

"Only if you expect old man Marchandt to ante up
the capital we need to stay in business." Henderson
stuffed the documents into his briefcase. "You're
thirty-six-years old. A man's gotta do what a man's
gotta do."

"If I require a wife and child, I'll simply borrow
yours."

Henderson smiled. "Oddly enough, I'm not willing
to lend them. Despite all my whining about the chaos
and frustration married life heaps upon my pitifully inadequate shoulders, I wouldn't trade my family for all
the world's riches." Snapping the briefcase shut, he
rose, his smile widening into a grin. "Now, season
tickets for the Mets I might consider."

"I'll keep that in mind." Royce stood, then escorted
his valued friend and associate to the study door.
"Meanwhile, put out the feelers on another capital investment firm in case Marchandt pulls the plug on our
deal. The company can't afford to be caught in the
lurch on this one."

Henderson's grin faded, his eyes instantly reflecting
the seriousness of their financial situation. "I know."
He opened the study door and stepped into the spacious
hallway that opened into the foyer. "Thing is, I've al-

ready contacted every reputable firm in the—'' His gaze fell on a curly-haired toddler happily dancing circles on the gleaming marble floor. ''Well, what have we here?''

The baby, clad in a spotless corduroy jumper and tiny striped T-shirt, instantly spun around, jammed his fingers in his mouth and drooled all over his hand. He giggled up at Royce. ''Daddy!''

Henderson blinked, rocked back on his heels. ''You've been holding out on me.''

Royce groaned. ''The child is mistaken, of course.''

''Of course,'' Henderson agreed with only the slightest trace of a smile. ''Looks just like you, too. Brown eyes, dark, curly hair. Talk about a baby of convenience. Marchandt will love him.''

Clasping his hands behind his back, Royce cleared his throat and spoke to the bright-eyed youngster. ''I am not your father, young man.''

''Uh-huh.''

The baby giggled again, a high-pitched, childish chuckle that sent a peculiar warmth down Royce's spine. It was an infectious laugh, one issued with such unabashed joy that Royce felt his own lips curve in response.

''Kitty has babies,'' the toddler announced.

''Indeed.'' A quick glance confirmed that the basement door was open, evidence that the attractive Ms. Michaels was currently tending the mewling brood.

Beside him, Henderson's slumped shoulders had squared, and eyes that had moments ago been sluggish with fatigue now sparkled with interest. ''Kittens? Pets *and* a child? This is perfect, absolutely perfect. Now all you need is a...''

His voice trailed off as a beautiful blonde emerged

from the basement, her frantic gaze darting around the immaculate room.

"Ask and ye shall receive," Henderson mumbled reverently.

Laura Michaels's head snapped around. She blinked at the two men, saw her son and issued a pained sigh. "There you are." She hurried over and scooped the baby into her arms, apologizing profusely. "I'm so sorry, Mr. Burton. I just turned my back for a moment, but you know how children are."

"No, as a matter of fact I don't."

Royce was fascinated by a peculiar dimple at the corner of her mouth that twitched when she spoke. It was oddly attractive, providing a focal point beside lips that were fuller than average, and exceedingly shapely.

When her tongue darted out to moisten them, an unexpected throb tightened his belly. He yanked his gaze to her eyes, which were riveted on him with cloudy confusion.

Since he hadn't heard the doorbell, he presumed she'd used the key Marta had reluctantly provided.

Royce cleared his throat again, clasped his hands behind his back. "The, er, animals... They are doing well?"

"Yes, thank you." She shifted the child in her arms, used her free hand to twist a honey-colored strand of hair behind her ear. The nervous gesture was one of habit, he suspected, as was the manner in which she scraped her lower lip with her teeth.

Assessing body language was a handy talent in Royce's business. Quirks, expressions, the smallest facial tics provided a wealth of information. The lovely Ms. Michaels was still dressed in the casual tank top and denim shorts she'd been wearing this morning when she'd first appeared on his porch searching for her wayward cat. She'd worn no makeup then, nor had she applied any for her late-afternoon visit. Clearly she'd made no attempt to attract his attention.

Not that additional effort would have been necessary. This was a naturally beautiful woman, one who needed no complement of cosmetics for enhancement. That wouldn't have been particularly telling, except that most women in Royce's world wouldn't have ventured from their boudoirs until they'd been properly painted, coiffed and bedecked in the finest designer fashions.

Caution was always prudent for a man in Royce's position. It wasn't arrogance that kept him on guard, merely the discretion born of unpleasant experience. He'd learned the hard way that it wasn't unusual for unmarried men of substantial means to be approached by females longing for a rich prince to whisk them away from laborious lives into a Cinderella castle gleaming with luxurious opulence.

There were usually clues, of course. A too-bright smile, eyes that were both hungry and hopeful, a sensual sway of a body too close to be appropriate, the constant touch of fingers brushing his wrist, his arm, his hand, probing for a response, for a hint of encouragement.

Laura Michaels revealed none of these traits. After retrieving her son, she'd stepped back, widening the space between them.

Her gaze was now guarded, her shoulders stiff and wary. She avoided eye contact, preferring a nervous sideways glance, after which her pale complexion tinted a delightful rosy pink at the cheekbones, and that funny dimple jittered like a bug on hot concrete.

This was not a woman trying to attract attention to herself. On the one hand, Royce was relieved by that. On the other, he was oddly deflated.

"I left the cats' food and water bowl behind some crates, where they'll hopefully be out of your way. I, ah—" she paused to skim a wary glance at Dave Henderson, who was grinning at her as if a gift bow had sprouted atop her head "—can't tell you how much Maggie and I appreciate your generosity."

Henderson's eyebrows shot toward his hairline. "Maggie? How many women do you have stuffed in the basement, anyway?"

The pink tint along Laura's cheekbones brightened to a vivid fuchsia.

"Maggie is my c-cat," she whispered with an embarrassed stutter. "She stubbornly transformed Mr. Burton's basement into a maternity ward, and he has been kind enough to allow me to tend the litter there until the kittens are old enough to leave their mother."

More annoyed by the unintended insult to Ms. Michaels than by his friend's thin attempt at humor, Royce cut him with a look that would have frozen most men to the bone.

Unmoved, Henderson merely smiled and thrust a beefy hand at the startled woman. "Dave Henderson, vice president and chief financial officer of Burton Technologies, Ms....?"

The woman licked her lips again, her gaze darting as if seeking escape. "Michaels," she said after a moment's hesitation. Juggling the baby to the crook of her left arm, she accepted Henderson's handshake. "Laura Michaels."

"Pleased to meet you. I hope you're finding the hospitality around this gleaming mausoleum to be adequate.''

Clearly uncomfortable, she edged a longing look toward the open basement door. ''Mr. Burton has been very kind.''

''Has he now?'' Grinning broadly, Henderson angled a smug glance, the meaning of which did not escape Royce's notice. ''Tell me about yourself, Ms. Michaels. Have you lived in Mill Creek long? What is your profession? How old is your son? Is your husband the jealous type?''

Her jaw dropped in shock. ''I beg your pardon?''

''Excuse us, Mr. Henderson was just leaving.'' Furious, Royce grabbed Henderson's elbow and hauled him toward the front door.

''She's perfect,'' Henderson whispered a moment before Royce shoved him onto the front porch. ''I'll do some checking into her family's background, and see what kind of financial arrangements—''

Royce closed the door in his face.

Hovering at the massive carved entry for several seconds, he took a deep breath and tried to formulate an apology that he never had the opportunity to issue.

When he turned around, the foyer was empty. Laura Michaels was gone.

''Feel how soft he is,'' she murmured, palming the warm ball of white fluff. ''Look, she's trying to open her little eyes.''

Jamie widened his eyes, curled his small mouth into an O as he reached a flat, stiff baby hand out to pat the kitten's fluffy head. ''Tickles,'' he announced, snatching his hand back. He giggled, then thrust out both hands. ''Me hold.''

"Let Mama hold the kitten until he gets bigger, sweetie. He's very fragile right now."

Thwarted, Jamie scowled and turned his attention toward the wriggling, mewing mass of adorable kittenhood in the straw nest Maggie had chosen for her brood.

"Me want him," the baby announced, pointing to a mottled orange-and-white tabby whose coloring most resembled his mother's. "Him Sam."

"Sam, is it? A fine name." She laid the white kitten with the soft, angoralike fur back into the nest. "What about this one, sweetie? What shall we name her?"

Laura had no idea if the tiny animal was male or female, since pronouncing the gender of such tiny kittens was difficult even for experts. Still, there was a definitive feminine aura about the precious ball of fluff. "She feels like a fuzzy little bunny rabbit, doesn't she?"

Jamie nodded so hard he nearly fell over. "Bunny," he chirped. "Bunny-Cat."

"All right then, Bunny-Cat it is." Smiling, she felt a nudge under her elbow. She absently stroked Maggie, who had finished her supper and wandered over to purr proudly. "Yes, you've done a wonderful job," Laura told the blinking mama cat. "A lovely family indeed."

Maggie licked her paw and proceeded to wash her face while Laura and Jamie continued to admire the kittens.

Along with Sam and Bunny-Cat there was a particularly vocal gray-and-white kitten that Laura dubbed Rascal, a black kitten with a white, tuxedolike bib that she called Cary Grant, and the runt of the litter, a diminutive calico with a quiltlike coat that begged the name Patches.

Jamie was enthralled with each and every one of them. "Bunny-Cat," he murmured, snatching the white kitten before Laura could stop him. The kitten squeaked a protest as Jamie smacked a juicy kiss on its little head.

"Careful, sweetheart. They are too tiny to be handled much right now."

The baby giggled happily, issuing no protest as she retrieved the squirming kitten from his grasp, and returned it to the nest. Despite her caution about handling them, she couldn't keep herself from stroking each of the adorable animals, brushing a tiny ear with her knuckle, lifting a miniature paw with her fingertip.

Laura had always loved animals. She'd never had pets as a child. Her struggling single mom had barely been able to support Laura and her two sisters, let alone keep hungry animals well-fed and cared-for.

"Animals are like children in fur suits," she'd once told a sobbing Laura, who'd brought home a puppy she wanted desperately to keep. "They are a big responsibility. Yes, they make us happy. But unless we can make them happy as well, it's not fair of us to keep them from a good home where they'll have enough to eat and a big yard to play in."

Laura had understood. Kind of. But she'd never forgotten the agony of carrying that sweet, warm bundle from house to house until a kindly older woman took the puppy in, promising to give him a good home.

It had been the first time Laura had experienced the exquisite pain of a broken heart. It had not been the last.

As she slid a gentle finger down Cary Grant's sleek black fur, a peculiar tingle warmed her spine. Beside her, Jamie issued a gleeful squeak, followed by a tickled laugh. She knew before she turned what she would see at the top of the stairs.

She wasn't disappointed.

He was standing there, magnificently silhouetted by the spray of daylight from the upstairs foyer. Outlined, the perfection of his form was even more evident. The strength of his shoulders, the taper of hips that were obviously slender beneath the concealing shape of his expertly tailored suit.

Perhaps it was the angle of her gaze focused upward that made him seem taller than she'd realized, with the top of his head appearing to be only inches below the crest of the doorway.

But it wasn't what she saw that affected her so deeply. It was what she felt, a radiating heat that she instinctively knew was emanating from his gaze. The aura was as tangible as a touch, and just as stirring. She didn't have to see his eyes to know that they were focused on her with an intensity that seemed to penetrate every molecule in her body.

She was frozen in place, unable to move, to speak, to tear her gaze away. From what seemed a great distance, she was aware of sounds in the room. Her son's laughter. Maggie's proud purr. Mingling mews from the nest of kittens. All were overshadowed by the pounding of her own heartbeat, the frantic swish of her own pulse.

Something pulled on the strap of her tank top. An insistent tug, then another. "Mama, Mama!" Jamie's voice broke the spell, releasing her from the mesmerizing presence at the top of the stairs. With some difficulty, she turned toward the toddler whose eyes were huge with exuberance. "Daddy's home!"

Her heart seemed to wedge itself at the base of her

throat, nearly choking her. The child was so desperate for a father that he consistently claimed any man who looked at him with kindness. "No, sweetie, that's not your daddy."

"Uh-huh," he insisted with a smug grin, his glowing gaze riveted upward. "*My* daddy."

A coolness swept her shoulders, as if a draft had slipped down the stairway. When she looked back, the doorway was empty. Royce Burton was gone, leaving nothing in his wake but her son's sparkling grin, and a residual tingle along her own spine.

It was happening all over again, she realized. And it terrified her.

Chapter Three

Laura arrived at the Burton home later than usual, dressed in a mortifying serving uniform and armed with a fresh bag of kitty kibble.

Embarrassed by the silly attire required by her new job at a fast-food restaurant across town, she was relieved that Marta didn't respond to her knock at the back door. Too bad the job at Quick 'n' Good Food Mart didn't work out. It was bad enough she had to board a public bus looking like a barn-dance escapee. The last thing she needed today was another run-in with a prune-faced shrew who treated Laura with veiled contempt at best, open hostility on her bad days.

And any day Marta laid eyes on Laura was a bad day.

Presuming the grumpy housekeeper was preoccupied elsewhere, Laura used her key to let herself into the immaculate kitchen.

Over the past few weeks, her life had disintegrated from merely chaotic to a crowded pressure pot of panic. Wendy's tiny mobile home seethed with noise, with frustration, with the stress of too many humans crowded into too little space. Jamie, who'd always been a happy, cheerful child, had become cranky from lack of sleep, since his nap times were routinely interrupted by the shrieks of his boisterous roommates, and the cacophony of a blaring television through paper-thin walls.

These twice-daily trips to care for Maggie's increasingly active brood served only to stir the melee, disturbing Laura on more than one level. Maggie's enigmatic landlord, for example. Laura had yet to figure the guy out. He was a thoroughly unpredictable sort whose myriad moods both perplexed and fascinated her.

On the one hand, Royce Burton segued quite nicely into her perception of the rich and privileged with an aloof arrogance she recognized from having lived among the elitist Michaels clan.

On the other hand, he seemed oddly concerned about the health and well-being of not only Laura and Jamie, but the animals he professed to despise as well.

He complained about the kittens' incessant mewing, yet had carpeted the entire basement to protect the tiny animals from the dampness of an increasing autumn chill. He seemed mightily irked by Jamie's insistence on calling him "Daddy," yet inevitably appeared in the study doorway to watch the child play with the shiny new toys that appeared like magic in the otherwise sterile mansion. He scowled at Laura as if her presence presented the world's biggest annoyance. Yet he made certain a veritable buffet of refreshments was available during her visits, despite his housekeeper's obvious distress at the additional effort required.

Apparently much of his business was conducted from his study, so he was frequently at home during the kitty-care visits Laura had managed to sandwich between employment interviews, child-care duties for Wendy's two boys and her own frantic quest to find a lawyer who didn't care about pesky details. Like being paid, for example.

The meager salary from the second-shift serving job she'd finally landed was a mere pittance compared to her debt.

Sighing, Laura juggled the five-pound bag of cat food under her arm, vaguely aware of a peculiar warm-wood scent that reminded her of the old lumberyard down the street. A glance around the spotless food preparation area revealed that the oven wasn't in use, nor was anything bubbling on the cookstove.

A peculiar whirring sound also caught her attention, along with a series of shuddering scrapes, thumps and other ominous noise emanating from deep within the house. She had no time for idle curiosity or speculation. She had less than fifteen minutes in which to feed the cats, head to the corner and catch her bus.

As she reached the foyer, the floor began to vibrate, and the strange whirring sound grew louder. The high-pitched hum was penetrated by a male voice shouting over the din. There was tension in that voice, and an unnerving sense of alarm.

And all the disquieting noise was coming from the cellar.

Instantly alarmed, Laura rushed forward to the open doorway just as a shadow from the stairway exploded into human form, blocking her view.

Marta's eyes were huge, frantic. "You see what you've done?"

Laura could see nothing beyond Marta's horrified expression and the frenzied fling of her arms.

"Everything is ruined, completely ruined!" A metallic shriek like a buzzsaw chewing steel horrified her. Marta jumped as if shot, then jittered around to shake her finger in Laura's face. "This is all your doing!"

Stunned, Laura could only press a palm to her chest and stammer, "Mine? How…why…?"

"Trouble, that's what you are. I knew it the minute I laid eyes on you." Her face contorted more with fear than fury, Marta bit her lower lip. Casting a woeful glance down at the pandemonium below, Marta pressed her knuckle against her quavering mouth. Her chin crumpled like crushed paper. Stifling a sob, she pushed past Laura and rushed toward the kitchen.

For the space of a heartbeat, Laura was frozen in shock. Then a male shout, sharp with tension and edged by fear, penetrated the chaotic noise. Something was terribly, terribly wrong.

"Maggie," Laura whispered.

Shifting the kibble bag, she hurried down the winding stairs. Her heart nearly stopped at the sight that greeted her.

The basement looked as if it had been bombed. Sawdust was everywhere. Loose bottles of wine, some of which were probably worth more than Laura's ancient automobile, had been haphazardly piled or rolled into a corner of the basement. Pieces from one of the expensive oak wine racks had been tossed around the carpeted floor like kindling.

A frantic shout from across the room redirected Laura's attention. "Is it loose yet?"

Two male figures were hunkered in the corner where the straw-padded kitten bed had once been.

One of the male figures, a beefy block of a man wielding a whirring circular saw, squatted on denim-clad haunches that were partially obscured by a belt of lumpy leather pouches bristling with tools. The other was bent at the waist, his upper torso in shadows, although Laura could see the outline of a shoulder, along with a flash of forearm exposed by the rolled-up shirt-sleeve.

Maggie paced beside the two men, tail flicking, eyes focused intently on the activity.

The beefy workman flipped off the whirring saw and sat back on his heels. It took a moment for Laura's ears to adjust to the near silence.

A peculiar muffled whine caught her attention a moment before the workman spoke. "This here rack is bolted to the floor, just like the last one."

"Rip it out," said the man in the shadows. The voice clearly belonged to Royce Burton, which was somewhat shocking to Laura since she'd never seen the immaculately tailored executive without a suit coat, let alone tieless, rumpled and with rolled-up shirtsleeves.

The workman shrugged. "Seems a shame. Might be able to punch a hole in the back of the rack instead of tearing out the sides of it."

"Too dangerous. We can't be certain exactly where it is."

Again Laura heard the peculiar muffled whine, which evoked an instant reaction in Maggie. The mama cat emitted a comforting trill and tried to poke her head into one of the openings of the rack from which the wine bottles had already been removed.

In the space of a heartbeat, Laura's blood ran cold

as she recognized the muted sound as the desperate mew of a trapped kitten.

More tiny cries emanated from a wooden barrel in the corner, a barrel over which a rumpled, yet recognizably expensive suit coat had been tossed. A thick coat of sawdust covered the ruined garment.

The workman shifted on his haunches, heaving a regretful sigh. "There oughta be some way to get that thing out without tearing up a thousand dollars' worth of custom-built racking."

"Just tear the damned thing out," Royce snapped. "And be quick about it."

Although Royce's face was still concealed behind the edge of the wine rack, his voice brooked no argument, and the workman offered none. The burly guy grunted, shrugged and fired up the circular saw. A moment later the blade chewed mercilessly into the hard oak, spewing sawdust into a choking cloud.

Laura just stood by the stairs, frozen in shock, fear and dismay. Every drop of moisture evaporated from her mouth as she sized up the situation and grasped the seriousness of it. One of Maggie's precious kittens was trapped behind that massive wine rack.

A single slip of the saw blade could prove disastrous. The kitten had apparently managed to wriggle into the narrow space between the rack and the wall, and had somehow become stuck there. Royce was directing that the side of the rack be destroyed to gain access to that airspace without risking injury to the tiny creature that was trapped there.

Maggie was clearly perturbed by her baby's predicament. The poor animal paced frantically, flicking her tail, her mouth opening repeatedly in what could be presumed to be a frenzied vocalization at the kitten's plight, although any sound the mama cat made was being drowned out by the din of the whirring blade.

A cloud of sawdust sent Laura into a convulsive coughing fit, which was also drowned out by the din. Neither Royce nor the busy workman had noticed her presence.

As Laura caught her breath and wiped her stinging eyes, Royce suddenly stepped out of the corner long enough to scoop up Maggie into his arms. He stroked the distressed feline with obvious fondness and appeared to be speaking to her. Whatever he said seemed to soothe Maggie. She immediately rubbed her forehead against Royce's chin and nestled comfortably against his chest, with her huge cat eyes focused on the busy workman.

Before Laura could digest this unexpected and decidedly peculiar development between her beloved Maggie and a man who had only a few short weeks ago confessed to having despised cats, the workman flipped off the saw and stood, rubbing the small of his back. "That oughta do it," he grumbled.

Instantly Royce returned Maggie to the floor. He grabbed hold of a loosened sideboard. Nails bent with a screech as he ripped the board out and tossed it into the growing pile of chewed oak.

Then he dropped to his knees, his upper torso hidden from view. A grunt emanated from the corner behind the partially disassembled wine rack. "That's it…come on, little guy…just another inch… Ow! Damned splinters."

The workman scratched himself. "Want me to try and tip the rack forward?"

"No, it's too heavy" came the muffled reply. "If you lose your grip, the kitten will be crushed."

Laura's stomach lurched at the thought. She pressed her knuckles against her mouth to keep from screaming out loud. The kittens were only a few weeks old, so tiny and helpless. They'd barely begun to totter out of the crate bed to explore their new surroundings. It hadn't occurred to her that there might be dangers lurking for curious baby kittens, just as there were for curious baby humans.

She'd certainly understood the need to childproof Jamie's surroundings, and had done so even before he'd learned to crawl on his own. Why on earth hadn't she checked the basement for hazards?

This was all her fault. If anything horrible happened to one of Maggie's babies, Laura would never forgive herself.

"Damn, he's really wedged in there," Royce muttered. "I can feel fur, but I can't get a grip— Wait a minute. He's wiggling toward me... Gotcha!" He crawled backward and flopped into a sitting position, grinning broadly at the mewing, gray-and-white kitten in his hand.

It was Rascal, of course. Tiny Mr. Trouble-with-a-tail himself. Laura should have known that if there was a single enticing hole within reach, Rascal would be the one to investigate.

Now the terrified kitten clung to Royce's shirt and frantically mewed in his face as if relaying every detail of his frightening ordeal.

Royce chuckled, seeming utterly unconcerned by the tiny claws shredding his expensive garment, or the ragged gash in the knee of his suit pants. "I imagine you are pleased to be out," he told the kitten. "I don't like tight, dark places myself."

Rascal emitted a sound halfway between a pleasant trill and an emphatic yowl.

"You're very welcome." Royce sat back on the filthy floor, allowing Maggie to crawl onto his lap and groom the face of her rescued kitten. "But the next time you notice an enticing crack between a cabinet and a wall, do us all a favor and ignore it."

The air Laura had been holding in her lungs escaped with a massive whoosh, alerting Royce to her presence. His head snapped up, his eyes widened. He stood immediately, unceremoniously dumping Maggie onto the floor while the kitten still hung from his shredded shirt.

Royce's brows crashed together in a frown that was supposed to be ominous, Laura presumed, but seemed more like embarrassment to her.

"Your animals have wreaked havoc on my life," he announced.

Startled by his strident tone, she annoyed herself by stammering. "I know... I'm so sorry."

He huffed a "harrumph," peeled the frightened kitten from his shirt and carried it to the coat-covered barrel. With deliberate care, he lifted the garment in a manner that forced the sawdust to float harmlessly to the floor before placing Rascal inside with his litter mates.

"I can't believe it," Laura murmured, realizing that the barrel was tall enough to keep the kittens from escaping, yet posed no obstacle to the agile Maggie, who immediately leapt inside to tend her brood. "You sacrificed your coat so the kittens would be protected from breathing the sawdust."

Royce straightened, shifted, then turned his attention to the workman. "Repair what you can and clean up the debris."

The workman rubbed his chin, slipping a shrewd glance from Royce to Laura then back again. "I charge double for after-hours work."

Laura's heart sank. She was clearly responsible for the workman's bill, however outrageous it ended up being. How she'd pay for that and the extensive damage the rescue effort had caused was beyond comprehension.

With some effort she squared her shoulders and spoke with more confidence than she felt. "Please forward the bill directly to me," she told the workman, then turned toward Royce. "I will, of course, pay all costs for repairing your wine racks as well and for restoring the cellar to its original condition."

Royce skimmed a glance in her direction, then refocused on the workman as if he hadn't even heard her. "Leave your invoice with Marta on the way out."

The workman's grin broadened. "Plus expenses, of course."

Royce's eyes narrowed. "What expenses?"

"Dulled a perfectly good saw blade cutting them bolts. And it's past suppertime. Union rules say I gotta have me a meal ticket if I work past suppertime."

"Fine," Royce snapped, then strode across the room, cupped a firm hand around Laura's elbow and ushered her up the basement stairs. When they'd reached the foyer, he glanced at the toys stacked neatly in the corner. "Where is the child?"

"My roommate watches Jamie while I'm at work."

"You have a job?"

The surprise in his voice annoyed her. "Most people do."

"Is that why you're wearing that disgusting ensemble?"

Peeved by his pompous expression, she hiked her chin as if she actually enjoyed flouncing around town in a fire-red miniskirt, fringed thigh-boots and an insultingly low-cut peasant blouse with a garish cartoon chicken embroidered on the bodice. "Actually, I thought it was a rather smashing fashion statement."

He squinted at the logo on her chest with obvious disdain, tipping his head forward to display flecks of sawdust in his mussed hair. "The Cluck House?"

She'd never seen Royce Burton when he hadn't been perfectly tailored and immaculately groomed. There was a peculiar appeal to his current untidy condition, a vaguely arousing image of how he might look having rolled out of bed, tousled and sated from a night of lovemaking.

The startling perception heated her skin, tumbled her stomach. She cleared her throat, pretended she couldn't feel the embarrassed flush crawling along her cheekbones. "It's a perfectly respectable restaurant and a perfectly respectable job. Not everyone is born rich and lucky, you know."

Something softened his eyes, just for a moment. "Yes," he murmured. "I know." He blinked, frowned, clasped his hands behind his back in the manner she'd come to recognize as one he used when enforcing his control over a given situation, even while wearing a stained shirt with claw marks and a pair of ripped slacks.

Again she was struck by the odd appeal of his disheveled appearance, a flawed vulnerability that seemed strangely revealing.

"Respectable or not," he said, "a woman who majored in constitutional law should not be costumed like a dance-hall floozy while serving fried poultry parts to the gastronomically challenged. It's beneath you."

"You are hardly in a position to tell me what kind of work I should or should not be doing. The hours are flexible, the pay is adequate and—" She frowned as the context of his statement sank in. "Wait just a darned minute. How do you know what my college major was?"

His gaze was insufferably smug. "I'm not in the habit of handing out keys to my home to people about whom I know nothing."

"You had me *investigated?*"

"Of course." He rolled the admission off his tongue with a startled blink, as if the question itself had been ridiculous. "I presume this, er, employment opportunity presented itself quite recently."

Very recently, since she'd had only a brief and haphazard training session yesterday afternoon. Tonight would be her first shift. Still, she stubbornly refused to give him the satisfaction of validating what he apparently already knew. "I have to leave now. Please be assured, however, that this discussion of clandestine background investigations is not over. Not by a long shot."

Mustering as much dignity as possible while festooned like a Halloween piñata, Laura spun on her spiky fringed boot heels and took two strides before Royce's soft voice stopped her.

"I believe you've already missed your bus."

A voice in her brain warned her not to ask. She ignored it, flung an astonished glance over her shoulder. "How do you know what bus I'm taking?" She turned around, planted her hands on her hips. "In fact, how do you know that I'm taking a bus at all? I do own a car, you know."

He shrugged. "Since that vehicle's transmission went out last week and it's currently lodged in the impound lot until the towing charges are paid, the presumption that you must rely upon public transportation isn't much of a stretch."

Alerted by a draft on her tongue, Laura closed her mouth and stared at him.

Apparently unaware of or unconcerned by her astonishment at the extent of his knowledge about her private life, Royce made a production of brushing dust from his palms. "You realize, of course, that a minimum-wage job can't possibly make a dent in the debt you now owe, nor allow you to save enough money to move into your own apartment before your roommate's husband returns from Alaska in December."

The room seemed to tilt, and Laura felt as if she couldn't catch her breath. She touched the wall to steady herself, waiting for her breathing to slow so she could speak. She hadn't told Royce where Wendy's husband was working, only that he was on a temporary assignment out of the state. Nor had she told him or anyone else when Daniel Wyatt would be returning, since she hadn't known that information herself.

She lifted her chin, making a production of glancing around, as if sizing up her financial obligation rather than mustering a modicum of dignity. "Since you clearly know a great deal about me that is quite frankly none of your business, you must also be aware that I have no other options at the moment."

"Oh, but you do." He paused, frowning at his stained palms for a moment, although Laura suspected that he wasn't even seeing them, simply using the gesture to gather his thoughts. "Fortunately, I'm able to offer you a position that will allow you to use your talents and experience to their fullest advantage."

Her heart leapt, then pounded with increased intensity. This was, after all, a man who controlled the largest industry and highest number of available jobs in the entire town, if not the entire county. Not only was Burton Technologies renowned for offering above-market salaries and generous benefits, but for job security as well. Employees considered themselves to be part of the Burton family. Most expected to spend their entire careers there, and since the company prided itself on having never laid off a single worker in its twelve-year existence, the expectation of a long, bright future for those who were a part of the said family seemed a realistic one.

Which is why job openings were as rare as hens' teeth, and coveted like gold. Laura's application for employment had been placed on a waiting list along with a hundred other hopefuls.

She replied cautiously but couldn't prevent a touch of breathless anxiety. "If there is a position in your company for which I qualify, I'd be most pleased to consider any offer."

"At my company?" Frowning, he shook his head. "Staffing matters are handled by the personnel department. I don't bother myself with those details."

Hope crashed, dragging the walls of her stomach down with it. "I misunderstood. I thought you had a position available."

"I do. Are you interested?"

Now she was thoroughly confused, and more than a little suspicious. "That depends. Exactly what does this job require, and what do you expect of my job performance?''

''The job requires you to marry me. The duties would be—'' he looked her straight in the eye with only the trace of a smile ''—wifely.''

''What a pig.'' Tucking a hank of stick-straight brown hair behind her ear, Wendy kicked a rock beside the park bench. ''Honestly, Laura, I can't figure out why you are such a magnet for egomaniacal lunatics with swollen checkbooks and heads to match. It must be that Cinderella complex of yours. You keep looking for your prince.''

''I do not.''

''Sure you do.'' A screech from the playground across the lush grounds caught Wendy's attention. ''Danny, quit hogging the slide!''

The youngest Wyatt, a mischievous six-year-old whose greatest joy in life was tormenting his older brother, grinned amiably, then slid down the slick curving loop, freeing it for use by his frustrated sibling, along with the impatient line of youngsters queued behind him.

At the same moment, Jamie tugged on Laura's hand. ''Me wanna swing.'' Grunting madly, he pointed to the apparatus in question, as if unsure his doddering mother could recall what a swing looked like. His tiny forehead furrowed with such intensity that Laura couldn't help but smile.

''Okay, sweetums, but all the swings are full now. You'll have to wait your turn.''

Jamie pushed out his lower lip, appeared to be considering the wisdom of a full-size tantrum when something even more exciting than the playground swing set caught his eye. "Mewwy-go-round! Wanna go on the mewwy-go-round, Mama!"

The equipment to which he referred was not a colorful, musical carousel on which delighted youngsters straddled brilliantly carved animals. Rather, it was a flat steel pancake on which grinning children sat while indulgent parents used the tubular handholds to spin their offspring into a state of gill-green nausea. "Are you sure you wouldn't rather wait for a swing? I'm sure one will be available soon."

"Mewwy-go-round," the toddler chortled, clinging to her with both of his chubby hands and heaving himself backward until his small body was perpendicular to the ground.

Reluctantly Laura gave in, and allowed herself to be yanked toward the coveted prize.

Wendy chuckled. "What a wuss you are. If you keep spoiling him, you'll end up with a carbon copy of my two terrors."

Since Laura adored Wendy's sons, she took no umbrage at the comment. "I certainly hope so. Danny and Tim are two of the happiest, most well-adjusted kids I know."

"They fight all the time." Wendy, who'd been an only child, frequently fretted about her sons' boisterous nature.

"They argue. There's a difference." She lifted Jamie onto the corrugated flat surface, next to a handhold at the center. "My sisters and I argued, too. The older we got, the more we had to argue about. But we loved one another beyond reason."

"It's a shame you don't live closer to them. You seem to miss them so much."

Stepping back, Laura gave a gentle push, and the

unit slowly revolved. "We keep in touch, particularly Catrina and I. Our lives seem to be in parallel, actually, even though I'm the eldest and she's the youngest of the crazy Mitchell clan. Susan was always the logical one. She used to shake her head as we hung posters of the latest teen heartthrob, then she'd sit us down and read Gloria Steinem quotes to us."

Wendy laughed. "A radical women's libber, huh?"

"Well, I thought so at the time. Actually, Susan was just so incredibly self-reliant and unbelievably popular with the boys. She always had more dates than Catrina or I, which ticked us off because she clearly didn't need male approval for her self-esteem, and we did. It didn't seem fair somehow." Smiling, Laura gave the lazy flat wheel another push and felt a surge of admiration for Susan, who was happily teaching fifth-graders somewhere in Montana cow country. "In hindsight, I think the boys were drawn to her confidence, her sense of humor and the fact that she wasn't desperate for their attention. Not to mention that she was the prettiest girl in school."

"Not prettier than you, surely."

"Me? Oh, heavens, I was the homeliest kid in my class. To this day, I still see braces and baby fat every time I look in the mirror."

Wendy huffed and folded her arms. After a quick glance to check on her own boys, who were happily engrossed in a game of tag with several other children, she returned her full attention to Laura. "I can guarantee you that when men look at you now, they are not seeing braces and baby fat. As for that 'needing male approval' crud, I sure hope you're over that, or I'll have to hurt you."

A snicker slipped out, much to Laura's relief, since

she didn't want Wendy or anyone else to know how deeply wounded she'd been by the disillusionment of her first marriage. "I'm over it, all right. Jamie is the only man in my life, and that is exactly the way I like it."

"Spoken like a true, doting mom." Wendy patted her shoulder. "Which is no doubt why you told Royce Burton where he could shove that disgusting proposition of his."

Puffing her cheeks, Laura blew out a breath. "In all fairness, it was a business proposal, nothing more."

"Yeah, right." Wendy emphasized her disbelief with a rude sound. "Any time a man wants you to move into his house and play wifey, he's got more than business on his mind."

"Ordinarily, I might agree with you, but Royce—"

"Royce?" Wendy narrowed her eyes, causing Laura to guiltily avert hers. "Since when are you two on a first-name basis?"

Laura cleared her throat, stopped the revolving apparatus and helped Jamie, who was looking a bit peaked, scramble onto the grass. "Go play with Tim and Danny," she told the toddler, who nodded amiably and wandered toward his two playmates, who were roughhousing only a few yards away. When her son was out of hearing range, she turned toward her friend. "What are you going to tell Daniel when he shows up in two months and finds his kids relegated to the sofa?"

Wendy's eyes widened. "How did you know Daniel will be home in December?"

"I have my sources." Laura angled a glance. "It's true, isn't it?"

Wendy nodded, looking away. "I'm sure you'll have found someplace else by then."

"How? With money saved from a part-time, minimum-wage job?"

"Something else might come up."

"You don't believe that any more than I do."

Wendy shrugged. "Then you'll stay with us until something does come up. Daniel's a good man. He wouldn't even think of kicking you and Jamie into the street."

"I know that, hon." Touched, she hugged her friend and fought a swelling of grateful tears. "You're both good people. You'd sacrifice anything for Jamie and me. The point is that you shouldn't have to." She sniffed, stepped back and watched her beloved son playing with the older boys. "You've already done too much."

Wendy regarded her skeptically. "I presume you properly turned that Burton cad from a baritone into a soprano for insulting you with such a crude proposition."

"I told you, it was strictly a business proposal. Jamie and I would live in luxury for a few months, and he would get a fake family to show off in front of some stodgy European capitalist."

"Which you told him was totally insulting and unacceptable."

"Of course."

"And you further added that you'd have nothing to do with anything so underhanded, sneaky and immoral."

"My words exactly."

With an approving nod, Wendy issued a sigh of relief, only to glance over a moment later. "Oh, God. You're picking at a thread."

"Umm?" Laura glanced down and saw her busy fingers absently unraveling the hem of her knit shirt. With some effort, she balled her fists and thrust them behind her. "No, I'm not."

Horrified, Wendy spun around and grabbed her shoulder. "Yes, you were, you were thread-picking. You always thread-pick when you're hiding something."

"No, I don't," she lied, scraping her lower lip with her teeth.

"Lip-biting!" Wendy pointed at her mouth. "Thread-plucking *and* lip-biting. I knew it, I knew it, you're hiding something."

"Wendy, I—"

"Oh, my God, you're pregnant!"

"Good grief!" Yanking away, she stared in horror. "I am not pregnant. Immaculate conception has already been done."

"Then what is it?"

Heaving a sigh, Laura massaged her aching forehead. "Royce promised me a lawyer."

Wendy blinked. "A lawyer?"

"Yes, a top-notch custody attorney who could go head-to-head with any shark the Michaelses can afford."

Clearly bewildered, Wendy stumbled back a step, folded her arms and stared at Laura as if she'd suddenly grown antlers. "Why on earth did you tell him that the Michaelses were trying to get custody of Jamie?"

"I didn't tell him, he found out on his own."

"How?"

Laura tossed up her hands. "The same way he found

out that my ex-husband was living in Sweden with a transsexual belly dancer, I suppose. I have no idea where he gets his information, or how he knows what he knows. Royce Burton seems to have eyes all over the world. He's probably even got a report detailing your fetish for pansy-decal sleepwear.''

"Hey, pansies are perfectly noble flowers—" She blinked. "Your ex ended up with a transsexual belly dancer?"

"Apparently Donald doesn't know about the transsexual part."

A satisfied smile curved Wendy's lips. "I'd give every pansy nightgown I own to see the look on that rat's face when he finds out his new squeeze was born a mister instead of a miss."

Truth be told, so would Laura, although she flicked the topic away as if it were a pesky fly. "The point is, Royce has connections everywhere. He knows everything about me, including how much money I owe, and who I owe it to."

"That's an invasion of your privacy!"

"It certainly is."

"If he's been investigating my pansy sleepwear, it's an invasion of my privacy as well!"

"Indeed."

"I hope you told that louse in no uncertain terms what you thought of his sneaky, underhanded behavior."

"I did."

"And I hope you gave his 'business proposal' the succinct answer it deserved."

Laura stifled a cough. "Of course."

"Well." Wendy sucked a breath, expelled it all at

once and turned on her brightest smile. "I'm glad that's settled."

"Me, too." Pausing a beat, Laura tugged at the loose thread until half her shirt hem had unraveled. "So, do you have any big plans for Saturday morning?"

"Saturday? No, I don't think so." Her astute gaze settled on Laura's nervous fingers. "You're getting married, aren't you."

"Yes."

Wendy shrugged. "If someone offered me a free lawyer to help protect my son, I'd marry him, too."

Chapter Four

It was heaven. Sheer bliss, a brilliant, sunlit room decorated with bold colors and cheery wall plaques, more spacious than the entire mobile home that had housed five people.

Stunned, Laura could only stand in the doorway, speechless.

Jamie suffered no such impediment. Babbling madly, he dashed from the vividly enameled racks bursting with new toys to the miniature table and chairs, to the adorable, fire-engine red bed shaped like a race car that was the centerpiece of the impressive decor.

"Look, Mama, look! A sleepy car!" He flopped onto the mattress, giggling wildly, then scootched onto his knees, grasping a plastic steering wheel that made vroom-vroom sounds when twisted by small hands. Jamie was delighted. "I dwiving!" He poked a circular plastic disk in the center of the wheel, chortling as the bed issued a gooselike honk, which so thrilled him that he repeated the process until Laura snapped out of her shocked state to cross the room and pry his tiny fingers from the wheel.

"That's enough horn-honking, sweetie. Would you like to help Mama unpack your suitcases so we can put your clothes away?"

"Okay." The child scampered off the bed and dashed across the room to the closet, which was large enough to accommodate the belongings of a small army. A unit of drawers had been built into the mammoth storage area, along with racks and shelving units low enough for a child to reach.

It was a cathedral for clothing. Laura just gaped, realizing that her son didn't have enough possessions to fill even a tiny corner of the huge space.

A voice from the doorway startled her. "I trust the child's quarters are satisfactory?"

Laura spun around, saw Royce standing there, hands clasped behind his back, still garbed in the sleek gray suit and burgundy silk tie he'd worn for this morning's ceremony. "Ah, yes, it's—"

"Daddy!" Jamie let out a joyful whoop, and he would have dashed across the room if his toddler feet hadn't wrapped around themselves, causing him to stumble.

Laura moved quickly, lifted the child to his feet, grateful he was too fried with excitement to notice a small carpet burn on his fat little knee. "Mr. Burton is not your daddy, sweetheart."

"Please don't correct the child," Royce said. "His misdirection of the paternal title will only make our, ah, familial relationship seem more genuine."

That didn't set well with Laura. "It will only confuse him."

Royce shrugged. "Children are resilient creatures. Most sadly accept the fact that fathers come into their lives and leave just as quickly. His belief that I have momentarily taken over that role is quite convenient. It suits my purpose."

"It doesn't suit my purpose, Mr. Burton. I prefer to be honest with my son."

A twinkle of jaded amusement sparked his gaze, along with a twitch at the corner of his mouth that gave her pause. "I see. So how does a mother honestly explain how she is pretending to be a wife to a man she barely knows at the same time she rebukes her child for pretending that same man is his father?"

Laura felt the blood drain from her face. "Touché."

His gaze softened as he glanced away. "Our agreement suits both of us, Ms. Michaels. If not for the child, my needs would not be served, and you certainly would not have been desperate enough to become a part of it. So whether you like it or not, the child is—"

"Jamie," she snapped, shaken by the reality of Royce's bland observations. "His name is Jamie."

Royce glanced over and issued a slow nod. "Jamie is an integral part of our arrangement."

"Your point is taken, Mr. Burton." She squared her shoulders, embarrassed by having been reminded of the obvious.

Royce sauntered over to the sparkling new shelves heaped with sparkling new toys. He lifted a tiny truck, eyeing it with peculiar reverence. "It puzzles me that your son is frightened by gruff masculine voices on the one hand, yet claims a man he barely knows as his father."

"It's a long story."

"I have time."

She hesitated, then figured if she didn't tell Royce what he wanted to know, he'd just pick up a phone and call his handy-dandy, privacy-invading investigator. "Jamie is frightened of loud male voices because that's what he heard at his grandparents' home. The Michaelses may be quite proper in public, but in private they are a bunch of brawling lunatics. Adults screaming at each other make him cry."

A flash of empathy warmed Royce's gaze for a brief moment. "So why does he claim strange men as his father?"

"Once when Timmy Wyatt was talking about his daddy, Jamie asked what a daddy was." Tears leaked into her eyes at the remembered pain of realizing that her precious child did not even know what a father was. It had upset Laura then. It upset her now. Annoyed, she swiped at the moisture. "Timmy told him that a daddy was a nice man who smiled at you even when you were bad, and who loved you no matter what. So every time Jamie sees a man he considers to be nice, he calls him 'Daddy.'"

Something cracked in Royce's gaze then, a distant pain that was too muted to be defined, too obvious to be ignored.

On cue, Jamie leapt from the bed and scampered across the room to tug on Royce's sleeve. "Come see, Daddy. Me got sleepy car!"

"So you do." The curve of a smile on Royce's lips was vaguely discernible as he watched the toddler crawl onto the apparatus, and promptly demonstrate a vroom-vroom and a series of teeth-grinding honks.

Royce didn't seem the least bit perturbed by the

noise. "It would appear that the primary occupant seems pleased with the presentation."

"The room is beautiful," Laura murmured, irked by a peculiar weakness in her knees when he strolled over to stand beside her. He was close.

Too close.

As close as he'd been this morning, during a succinct ceremony that resembled a business meeting more than a wedding. Held in the antique-studded parlor, the brief service had been conducted by a judge who was introduced as a friend and associate of Royce's. There had been several gray-suited witnesses, along with Wendy and her sons. A few words had been spoken. Laura vaguely recalled mumbling in agreement when she'd been nudged to do so.

A ring of staggering beauty, studded with more diamonds than she'd ever seen mounted in such a small space, had been slipped onto her finger with no more elegance than one might use to apply a Band-Aid to a superficial cut.

Then Royce had thanked the judge, chivalrously escorted Wendy to a buffet of refreshments, then huddled with his stiff-backed minions in the study, supposedly to put the finishing touches on the Document of Dissolution and financial contracts that Laura had dizzily approved earlier in the week. All in all, the wedding had been less personal than the average corporate board meeting.

Except for those brief moments when Laura and Royce had stood together to exchange vows, when his scent had wafted around her like a protecting arm, and the soft brush of his sleeve had raised gooseflesh on her bare arm. Something had happened in those brief seconds, something that had shaken her soul, jarred her to the marrow.

Laura had frequently experienced odd physical sensations when Royce appeared. A peculiar rhythm in her heartbeat, a jittery pulse. But this morning had been the first time in her life that the sight of a human male had made her legs wriggle like limp noodles.

Now it was happening again, for no other reason than his benign presence. She chalked it up to nerves. It wasn't every day a woman got married, after all, even if the marriage itself was purely a business arrangement.

Peculiar heat radiated down her spine as his scent continued to tease her, wafting a unique blend of herbs and citrus that was subtle, yet erotically masculine.

Distressed by his continued effect on her, she stepped away, distancing them. "It certainly wasn't necessary to prepare something so…extravagant for Jamie's room. We're only going to be here for a few months."

Royce had scrupulously avoided eye contact with Laura during the ceremony, but he looked at her now, focusing with a gaze so intense that the roof of her mouth went dry in response.

"Accommodations needn't be Spartan simply because they are temporary." A touch of haughty condescension in his voice cut her to the quick. "I'm well aware that the primitive lifestyle you've been forced to endure recently is not of your choosing, nor does it suit your personal taste."

A flush of embarrassment announced itself by a creeping warmth along her jaw. "I resent the implication that worth as a parent is measured by and proportional to one's ability to supply material luxuries."

His gaze didn't waver. "Of course not. I apologize if you believed that was what I meant."

"I'm not sure what you meant."

He studied her with unnerving intensity. "As you are no doubt aware, I've taken the liberty of researching your background quite thoroughly. Your father abandoned the family shortly after your sister, Susan, was born. You were barely four at the time. Later, your mother remarried a man whose credentials were, shall we say, embellished upon. After he also deserted the family, she divorced him, gave birth to your youngest sister, Catrina, and spent the remainder of her short life struggling to raise the three of you in a situation that can only be described as abject poverty." He paused a beat, gazed toward the dark-haired child who was still engrossed in vroom-vrooming the car-bed steering wheel. "Under such stressful circumstances, one can understand why you'd have been driven to seek out a married life of wealth and privilege."

Laura was not surprised at the extent of his knowledge about her past. She was, however, angered by having it laid out before her in such unflattering terms. "Are you suggesting that I only married Donald Michaels to get my greedy little hands on his money?"

"Of course not." The denial would have mollified her had he not added, "Donald Michaels had no money. It was his family's money you sought."

Unable to stifle a gasp, she balled her fists, spoke softly, in a voice quivering with muffled fury. "How dare you say such a thing? You know nothing about me, nothing about my marriage to Donald."

If Royce was perturbed by her anger, he concealed it, preferring instead to slip a hand into the pocket of his slacks and casually rock back on his heels as if waiting for valet service beneath the awning of a five-star restaurant. "By all accounts, Donald Michaels is a spoiled, childish and selfish young man who has never worked a day in his life. I find it difficult to believe a woman of your obvious intelligence, maturity and appealing beauty would have been drawn to such a man if he'd been of average means."

For a moment, Laura was utterly speechless. Anger drained out of her as quickly as it had formed, which was as surprising to her as was Royce Burton's impudent assessment of her motives for her marriage into the Michaels family.

In reality, his perspective differed little from that of her in-laws, and of the world at large, for that matter. Few people had understood the vulnerability Laura had seen in a sad young man overshadowed by a domineering mother and an emotionless father whose approval he'd so desperately craved but had never received.

Donald was a lost soul, adrift in a world that callously refused to accept any man who hadn't learned to accept himself. His plight had touched Laura, changed her in ways so profound she still didn't understand what had happened to her. For the first time in her life, she'd found someone lonelier than herself, someone who'd actually needed her.

Eventually she had discovered the folly of committing her life to a man too emotionally scarred and immature to return the favor. By then, it had been too late.

Royce spoke, yanking her attention from the sadness of the past to the uncertainty of the present. "Please understand, I'm not judging the choices you've made, nor the reasons you've made them. I certainly appreciate the importance of money, and the desperation of not having it. Selecting a mate based on financial security is quite common, actually, and socially acceptable. You needn't be ashamed of it.''

There was no need to argue the point. Royce Burton was not, Laura suspected, a man prone to revising his esteemed opinion based on the pesky fact that he was dead wrong. She indulged herself with a sigh, absently massaged her eyelids, only to note with some irritation a teal stain on her fingers, and recall that she'd applied eyeshadow for the momentous occasion. She probably looked like an exhausted raccoon by now, but didn't much care. There was no reason to care what Royce Burton thought of her, no reason to allow his opinion to dampen her spirits or cause her to dwell on the unpleasantness of the past.

''Believe what you like, Mr. Burton. I suspect you will, anyway.''

He regarded her for a moment, as if assessing the acuity of her comment. ''Perhaps you should address me in a less formal manner. A wife's use of her husband's surname was commonly acceptable in Victorian times, although nowadays it tends to garner unwanted attention.''

His patronizing tone continued to irk her. She responded with a silky smile. ''Fine. How about 'sweet cheeks'?''

''That's charming, of course, but a simple 'Royce' will do nicely.''

''You, sir, are a humorless spoilsport.''

''I can live with that.''

''I can't.''

Startled, he hiked a brow, revealing a touch of confusion before a shuttered gaze erased all hint of emo-

tion. ''I must remind you that the documents you
signed specify significant financial loss if you fail to
adhere to the strict terms of our agreement.''

''Oh, I'll live up to my part of the bargain, just as I
expect you to live up to yours.'' She offered a saccha-
rine smile. ''Particularly the clause in which you promise to supply whatever support is necessary to ensure
our safety and well-being. Laughter is an emotional
necessity. Therefore, I expect you to provide it.''

Clearly taken aback, he rubbed his chin briefly before clearing his throat and rocking back on his heels.
''That clause referred specifically to physical needs,
such as food and medical attention.''

''The language of the contract makes no such dis-
tinction, a matter you can take up with your attorney
at a later time.'' She deliberately adjusted the magnificent diamond ring dwarfing her finger, then slid a
pointed glance toward the toddler who had abandoned
the car bed to explore a rack of colorful pull toys across
the room. ''Meanwhile, I expect you to smile in my
son's presence, force out a hearty chuckle when appropriate and provide a sterling example of a man who is
happy with himself and the life he has chosen.''

This time he made no attempt to conceal his shock.
''I am perfectly content with myself and my life.''

''I didn't say content. I said happy.'' Tilting her
head, she studied the creases beside his mouth, the constant wariness that draped his golden-brown eyes with
the drab essence of a man at war with himself. ''The
truth is that you are neither happy nor content, despite
your protestations to the contrary, which is your personal business, of course. However, children observe,
absorb and take personal responsibility for emotional
turmoil in their adult role models. I don't want my son

exposed to that. I would, therefore, appreciate your assistance in conducting yourself in a pleasant and jovial manner in his presence.''

''Jovial?'' He practically sputtered the word, much to Laura's delight. ''My good woman, I am not Santa Claus.''

''Tell that to Jamie.'' She jerked a thumb toward the happy toddler, who'd removed each of the bright new toys from the reachable racks and seemed overwhelmed by the sheer magnitude of his good fortune. ''I must insist that you tether your generosity and refrain from lavishing my son with a lifestyle I will not be able to maintain.''

He nodded, stone-faced. ''I understand. Locating new millionaires to marry will be difficult, considering the rate you've gone through them thus far.''

Now it was Laura's turn to sputter, until she noticed a subtle gleam of satisfaction in his eyes and the slight crinkle of a smile bend the corner of his mouth. ''If that was your best attempt at humor,'' she said with deliberate coolness, ''it needs a bit of refining.''

''I'll work on it.'' Then with a brusque nod, softened only by a subtle gleam in his eye, he exited the room.

A chill brushed her cheek, as if the warmth had been sucked from the room along with him. Laura absently rubbed her upper arms. Royce had been all too correct about his presumption that she'd entered this false marriage because of his money. If it took fire to fight fire, it took money to fight money.

Wealth represented safety, security. Royce Burton was rich enough and powerful enough to engage the Michaelses on their own turf. That was all that mattered. To keep from losing her son, and to provide the financial security needed to protect him from suffering the poverty of her own childhood, Laura would have married the devil himself.

A niggling voice in her mind suggested that might be exactly what she had done.

The seashell gleamed in his palm, polished hues of pearlescent pink and silver inside, a scallop of ivory grit on the outside. It was an ordinary shell, one of millions washed up on Hawaiian beaches each year, the sea-swept remnant of some long-lost creature, faintly scented by salty brine.

To Royce, it smelled like sweet lilac and nasturtium, the remnant of a long-lost dream. He still saw her in his mind, frolicking on the sunlit sand, her laugh echoing above all the others along the crowded Honolulu shore. She'd run barefoot through the surf, foam licking her slender ankles as she scooped a handful of the Pacific Ocean to playfully fling his way.

She'd found the shell buried in the damp sand, washed it off, dried it on the floral skirt he'd purchased for her at an outrageously expensive gift shop in Waikiki. It was the only gift she'd ever given him.

It was, in fact, the only personal gift he'd received since his mother's death. He didn't know why he'd kept it all these years. He only knew that he couldn't part with it, couldn't part with the memories.

Couldn't part with the pain.

A voice from the study's open doorway startled him. "She was a gold-digging tramp," Marta said. "Just like the one upstairs now."

Reflexively closing his fingers around the shell, he arranged his features to reveal nothing of his internal thoughts or emotions. "Ms. Michaels—" He caught himself, then issued a correction smoothly, without a shift in tone. "My wife is to be treated with the utmost courtesy and respect. You understand the reasons this is necessary, reasons that extend far beyond the convenience of any one person. Therefore, I trust you will adhere to my wishes in this matter."

Her mouth thinned, deepening a line of vertical creases gouged along her upper lip. "I understand more than you think I do."

Royce smiled. "I long ago learned never to underestimate you, Marta." He replaced the shell in a small wooden box, locked the box in the top drawer of his study desk and pocketed the key. "My mother trusted you, and so do I."

Sparse brows, reddish and thin, relaxed above the woman's still-wary eyes. "She would have been proud of all you've accomplished."

A pang of regret twisted deep in his chest. "Yes," he whispered. His achievements had come too late for the woman who had urged him to do great things with his life. "There's so much I could give her now, beautiful things, travel to places she'd only dreamed about."

Marta's expression softened. "She wouldn't have cared about your money. It's the success you've made of your life that would have pleased her."

The comment genuinely startled him. "One can hardly live in squalor and consider oneself to be successful. Wealth is the only true measure of success."

"Your mother would disagree."

A tightening in his chest forced him to draw a sharp breath. The conversation was veering into that long-ago place Royce didn't care to revisit. "You were my mother's dearest friend for the final years of her life, Marta. She cherished you, as do I. Her memory is precious to us both. Let's not taint it by discussing which of us best understood her innermost thoughts on such matters.''

The rebuke was softly issued, implicit in its meaning. Few people would dare challenge it. Marta was, and always had been, one of those few. ''It would hurt her to watch you being used again, and to see you allowing it. It hurts me, too. You're not a man prone to making the same mistake twice.''

''The situations are entirely different.''

''No, the situations are entirely the same. Two money-hungry women intent on getting their grubby fingers on your wallet. This one is even more despicable, because she's using a child to worm her way into your heart. A child!''

''That's enough, Marta.''

''I saw what you went through when you found out what kind of woman Sabrina was. I saw your pain, your heartbreak. Don't ask me to watch that happen all over again and be happy about it.''

Spinning where he stood, Royce turned toward her and slammed his fist on the desk. ''I am not asking, I am telling.''

His voice was low, deadly enough that Marta widened her eyes in real fear. That gave him no pleasure. It did, however, achieve the desired result. She snapped her lips together and was silent.

As Royce continued to speak, he saw the color drain from Marta's already pale face. ''You will treat Laura and her son as honored guests. You will attend to their needs, see to their comfort. Whether you like it or not, this will be their home for the next few months, and I will not have you making their stay here more difficult than it needs to be. This is not a request. It is a direct order." Laying his palms flat on the polished mahogany surface, he leaned over the desk, skewering her with a look. "Have I made myself clear?"

She issued a curt nod. "Perfectly."

"Good." He straightened, squaring his shoulders against a sudden slump of fatigue. "Please inform Ms. Mich—" He sighed, pinched the bridge of his nose. "Please inform my wife that dinner will be served at six o'clock. Offer her the option of sharing the meal with me or dining alone if that is her preference."

"Yes, sir." Clearly wounded by his rebuke, Marta blinked eyes that were a shade too bright. "And the child?"

"The child?" Royce frowned. He'd forgotten about little Jamie.

Clearing her throat, Marta spoke carefully. "The decor of the formal dining area does not lend itself to—" she fidgeted "—a toddler's lack of table manners."

He flinched at the image of his five-hundred-year-old Persian carpet stained with baby food. "I, er, presume she'd prefer to feed the child separately." This was growing more complicated by the moment. "Perhaps that would be best accomplished in the kitchen."

"I'll see to it."

Royce vaguely noted the satisfied smile curving the lines above her thin mouth, but was too emotionally exhausted to dwell on its meaning.

Once alone in the study, Royce crossed the room to collapse into his favorite chair, an oversize burgundy recliner nestled in a corner of floor-to-ceiling bookshelves. It was his thinking place, filled with the comforting scent of leather and lemon polish, and a potpourri of aromatic flowers from a floral arrangement Marta freshened daily.

He could allow his shoulders to soften now, allow his head to fall back against the supple, tufted headrest. There was no need to maintain a taut expression, or guard against the revealing spark of emotion in his eyes. He could permit the anguish to show on his face, in his gaze. There was no one to see it.

Alone in this private corner of a mansion that was in some ways still foreign to him, Royce was free of his self-imposed exile. He could be the man he wouldn't permit the world to know, the man he'd struggled a lifetime to suppress. This was where he faced his insecurity, pondered mistakes he refused to publicly acknowledge. Memories haunted him here, curling like smoke through a troubled mind. In this peaceful, quiet place, he could accept the reality of who he was. He could accept the loneliness.

He just couldn't accept the fear.

Chapter Five

Prowling beyond the darkened stairs, Laura tiptoed past the short hallway leading to Marta's quarters. The last thing she wanted was to awaken a person who never missed an opportunity to point out what a distasteful burden Laura's presence had created.

Balancing two steaming mugs of hot chocolate, Laura slipped silently toward the light emanating from the study wing of the massive home.

A voice filtered from the study, firm and efficient. "Capital expansion will give us the international recognition we need to capture a profitable share of the foreign market," Royce was saying. He paused a beat. "Hmm? Yes, I'm aware there is a risk involved. No challenge is met without a price."

Laura hesitated, suddenly unsure of a mission she'd repeatedly replayed in her mind. She knew Royce's habit was to work late into the night, frequently holding telephone conferences with international colleagues for whom an ungodly hour on this continent coincided with a normal business day on theirs.

Over the past week, she'd covertly observed a schedule strenuous enough to fell a lesser man. Royce was still an enigma to her, seemingly unimpressed by the power he wielded both as an executive and as a man.

Despite an outer display of supreme confidence, a hint of veiled insecurity occasionally crept into his gaze, particularly when unaware he was being observed. That intrigued Laura.

It also unnerved her. There was something innately appealing about the elusive Mr. Burton. Laura was fascinated by the dichotomy he posed. On the one hand, the ease with which he made decisions with life-shattering consequence for thousands of hard-working people confirmed her previous experience with the rich and the powerful. As part of the dysfunctional Michaels clan, Laura had been privy to family secrets, hidden agendas and clandestine meetings designed to consolidate family power at the expense of others.

On the other hand, Royce was not as harsh as he'd like the world to believe. Yesterday, for example, Laura had walked into the kitchen to see him smiling wistfully through the window, watching Jamie play in the yard. Clearly distressed that she'd witnessed such an unguarded moment, he'd grumbled out of the room, complaining about an untidy scatter of toys marring his manicured landscape.

He was, she suspected, a man who had scrupulously reinvented himself for the world at large. She couldn't help but wonder why he'd felt that necessary. Despite her intention to maintain an emotional distance, she couldn't seem to keep herself from speculating about

Royce's elusive past, nor could she conceal the irksome physical reaction his presence elicited in her.

He was, as Wendy would say, a hunk and a half.

A tremor vibrated the hot liquid in both cups. She realized that her arms were quivering.

It wasn't fear that set her nerves on edge; it was anticipation, an anxiety that made her pulse race, her mouth twitch, her skin prickle with peculiar angst.

His voice sent a warm shiver down her spine. "Yes, yes, you're quite correct. I knew you'd understand."

For a moment, she considered a judicious retreat. Clearly he was on the telephone, since only one side of the conversation was audible. "It was, of course, the only prudent decision possible."

Mustering another ounce of courage, Laura took a calming breath, steadied the mugs of hot chocolate and continued toward the brightly lit study, reminding herself that she'd meticulously planned this moment by carefully mapping the time and place Royce would be most approachable.

Presuming, of course, that such an unpredictable man could ever be deemed approachable in the first place.

She peeked through the open doorway, saw the ripple of Royce's back muscles through the fine material of his expensive shirt. His suit jacket had been removed and hung on a wooden hanger, dangling from an antique coatrack on the far side of the room.

Royce himself was seated behind an exquisite desk of polished mahogany, facing the south window. He continued to murmur softly, clearly unaware of her presence. "I suppose it's selfish of me. Still, there are benefits for both of us, which is supposedly the hallmark of successful negotiation."

To Laura's surprise, the telephone was cradled on the desk, and he didn't appear to be holding the palm-size recorder into which he frequently dictated notes, memos and instructions to his staff. His right shoulder flexed, as if he was rhythmically shuffling something in his lap.

"What's that?" He tilted his head downward. "Oh, I sincerely doubt that. Hmm? Well, perhaps...we'll see."

In the doorway, Laura discreetly cleared her throat to announce her presence.

Royce swiveled around as if shot, gaping at her with such shock that she took a step backward, sloshing the contents of the mugs.

She cursed this man's uncanny ability to make her stammer repeatedly. "I—I'm sorry, I didn't mean to interrupt your conversation with—" a pair of perky yellow eyes peered over the edge of the desk "—with Maggie?"

Royce stood quickly, requiring the cat in question to leap from his lap to the floor. With an expression bordering between mortification and outrage, he drew in a breath, presumably preparing to dispute the ludicrous notion that he was carrying on a conversation with an animal. But no sound emerged.

After a despairing moment of silence, he simply snapped his mouth shut and glowered.

Blinking in disbelief, Laura watched her beloved feline stroll out from under the desk, hop into a burgundy armchair and proceed to groom herself with a complacency that implied surprising familiarity with the territory in question.

She found her voice before Royce found his. "What on earth is Maggie doing in here?"

Clearly nonplussed by the intrusion, Royce displayed a fierce frown Laura recognized as an expression of deliberate intimidation rather than genuine annoyance.

"The animal has developed an irksome habit of traveling wherever she wishes," he grumbled, directing a pointed gaze at Laura. "Not unlike its owner."

The unexpected sight of a self-confessed cat-hater carrying on a conversation with a contented feline nesting in his lap was startling enough for Laura to ignore the warning glint in Royce's eye.

"But the only way out of the basement is through the window into the yard." The window in question was kept ajar for Maggie's convenience, although the kittens were still too small to reach it. "There's no way she could get into the house unless someone opened a door for her."

Royce narrowed his gaze, clasped his hands behind his back. "Is there some reason you are prowling into my work space at this ungodly hour of the night? Besides the joy of simply irritating me, that is."

Maggie, having completed her toilette, cast an adoring glance at the rigid human behind the desk before curling into nap mode. Tufts of orange fur clinging to the cushions confirmed that this wasn't the animal's first visit to that particular chair. A startling realization struck her. "You let her in, didn't you?"

Clearly embarrassed, Royce blustered, coughed, turned slightly crimson. "It's the only way to silence her incessant mewling long enough to get any work done."

"Maggie does not mewl. She does, however, issue an occasional courteous request." Stifling a smile, Laura crossed the room, placed one mug on his desk, cradled the other between her palms. "I thought you might enjoy some hot chocolate, although it's probably cool chocolate by now."

He harrumphed, shuffled his feet and finally sat in his chair with a flounce not unlike that of a thwarted child. He slid a sideways glance toward the mug, angling his gaze slightly upward to include Laura, who stood on the other side of the desk. "Since you're here you might as well sit."

"Thank you."

She seated herself in one of several tapestry-upholstered guest chairs arranged throughout the study. A sip of chocolate confirmed that the beverage was lukewarm. A glance at the burgundy armchair confirmed that the normally cautious and cynical mama cat was dozing peacefully.

Laura balanced the mug on her knee. "I'm sorry Maggie has been such a bother to you. She usually doesn't intrude where she isn't wanted."

It was obvious Royce had invited Maggie to share his inner sanctum. It was just as obvious that he didn't want to confess to having done so.

Frowning, he tapped a pencil on his desk, appeared to be suddenly engrossed in scrutinizing a document in front of him. "Have you received the itinerary for next week's activities?"

Her throat went into spasms midswallow. It took a moment for her to arrange her features to express a calm she didn't feel. "Yes. As a matter of fact, there are some appointments scheduled that concern me."

"Oh?" He retrieved his mug, sipping the beverage without further comment.

Placing her own mug on the edge of his desk, she licked her lips, nervously smoothing the discreet lounging robe into which she'd changed after a grueling day in panty hose.

Part of their agreement had been that Laura would conduct herself in a manner appropriate to her status as wife of the town's wealthiest and most influential citizen. During the past week, she had dutifully attended a get-acquainted luncheon with the spouses of other Burton Technologies executives, presided over two charity fund-raisers and a tedious political rally where she'd presented the grateful candidate with a generous campaign contribution.

"Is there a problem with the number of appearances scheduled?" Royce asked.

"No, not really." Despite a full schedule, Laura had been able to spend a great deal more time with Jamie than she would have had she been forced to take a full-time job. "It's just that I noticed that I have...that is, we have an appointment next Thursday evening."

He regarded her thoughtfully. "The gallery opening."

"Yes." She allowed herself the luxury of another calming breath. "Thursday is soccer night."

A perplexed crease edged along his brow. "I wasn't aware you were such a soccer fan."

"Oh, I'm not. I mean, I love soccer, of course, but Thursday night's game has nothing to do with me. It's Wendy." She was rambling, she knew, but seemed unable to extricate herself without nattering on like a nervous schoolgirl.

Her voice rose to a high squeak that made her flinch. "Her boys play soccer. They're on the team. Well, not the same team, of course, since Timmy is nine and Danny is only six, but they play on the same night. At the park. There are several fields. Most of the league's teams play on Thursday. Some play on Friday. But Tim and Danny play on Thursday.''

Cringing at her foolish redundancy, Laura finally managed to clamp her mouth shut before more idiocy poured out.

Across the desk, Royce studied her with the guarded wariness of one witnessing a nervous breakdown in progress. ''I'm not sure I understand the connection, unless you'd rather observe your friend's children play soccer than adhere to your contracted commitments.''

Laura sighed. This was not going well. ''It's not the game, it's the fact that Wendy won't be available to watch Jamie that night.''

''Is the child-care facility I recommended unsatisfactory to you?''

''No, it's wonderful. Jamie loves it, but it closes at 6:00 p.m.'' She absently plucked a loose thread at the edge of the robe's silky sleeve. ''I was hoping you might be willing to attend the gallery cocktail party without me.''

''Your attendance is required,'' Royce said firmly. ''Marta will watch the child during our absence.'' Apparently Laura's attempt to stifle a grimace was unsuccessful. ''Is that a problem for you?''

Squirming in her chair, Laura reorganized her thoughts by gazing around the handsome room. Books adorned two walls, floor to ceiling, encompassing the burgundy chair on which Maggie now napped like loving, leather-scented arms. A vibrant bouquet of autumn foliage and fresh flowers spilled from a crystal vase nearby. An antique sideboard bristled with photographs, and a framed dollar bill, presumably the first earned by his now-thriving company.

Several watercolor landscapes of similar style were

grouped in a place of honor between huge carved book-cases. The paintings were pretty enough, although they seemed a bit unpolished, even amateurish. The signature of each was a set of initials, J.L.B., with the *B* cleverly evolving into a four-leaf clover, and the other two letters melting into a tangle of twisting ivy.

Laura actually liked the signature better than the paintings.

The sights slipped into her subconscious without fanfare as she struggled to choose her words. From behind the massive desk, Royce regarded her with an acuity she found unnerving.

"It would be unfair to impose upon Marta," she said finally. "Her responsibilities as cook, housekeeper and office assistant are exhausting enough without adding after-hours child care to her list of duties."

Sipping his chocolate, Royce appeared to consider that. Finally he set the mug aside. "Marta's responsibilities include whatever I require of her, for which she is well compensated. As are you, I might add."

She stiffened, feeling chastised for having questioned his authority. "I am a mother first, Mr. Burton, and your employee second. Our contract is quite clear about my priorities in that regard. The welfare of my child will always take precedence in my life."

"You feel that Marta endangers the welfare of your child?"

"Not at all. She has treated Jamie with tolerance and kindness." Which was surprisingly true, since she treated Laura as if she were the devil incarnate.

Fortunately, that obvious resentment did not appear to extend to Jamie. Marta spoiled the baby with freshly baked treats, removed fragile objects from his grasping hands gently, with the hint of a smile, and took pains to assure that the pantry was filled with his favorite snacks and beverages. "I simply don't want our presence to create more of a burden on her than it must."

"I see." Leaning back in the chair, Royce steepled his fingers. "Is that why you've insisted on preparing your own meals, taking care of your own laundry needs and refusing housekeeping assistance for the child's nursery, as well as your own quarters?"

Was there anything this man didn't know?

"It seems an appropriate accommodation." There was no reason to expand upon the unspoken agreement, which appeared to have mollified Marta's feelings of being put-upon, and alleviated at least some of Laura's own guilt at having caused extra work for the harried woman.

"I see." The intensity of his gaze unnerved her. "I hope you're more pleased with the legal assistance that has been supplied than you are with the housekeeping services."

She flushed, annoyed by her own emotional transparence. "The attorney you recommended is more than adequate. He has already drafted a notice to the Michaelses' lawyer, informing him that any attempt to gain legal custody of my son will result in a vigorous, lengthy and expensive defense, the cost of which they will be expected to bear. Since their primary basis for the matter, my financial inability to care for Jamie, has been resolved by our, ah, marriage, he believes that their attorney will recommend immediate withdrawal of the complaint."

The news appeared to please him. "Good."

"My attorney... That is, your attorney also believes that the clause in our prenuptial contract that assures me a regular income until Jamie is in school will prevent them from reimplementing the lawsuit after the marriage is dissolved.''

He nodded. ''Of course.''

''I can't thank you enough for your help, Mr.—'' she caught herself ''—Royce. You'll never know how much this means to me.''

Leaning forward, he nodded, acknowledging her gratitude. ''Successful negotiation brings something to the table for all participants. I live up to my part of the bargain, you live up to yours. It's simply a business arrangement, nothing more, nothing less.'' He shrugged, a dismissive gesture that didn't veil a subtle glow of relief in his own eyes.

At that moment, Laura realized that he, too, had been concerned about the custody matter, more concerned than he'd been willing to reveal.

At that moment the long-term income clause in their marriage contract took on a new meaning. Royce had immediately offered her an ongoing salary substantial enough that she'd be able to stay home with Jamie until he started school. He must have known she'd have accepted much less than that.

At the time, she'd been perplexed by his generosity, although deeply grateful for it. Now she realized that Royce had understood that without long-term economic stability, the Michaelses would be circling like vultures, ready to swoop in the moment Laura found herself alone and financially vulnerable.

He had quietly protected her future and had sought no recognition for the kindness. He cared, he actually cared. Although he'd probably deny it outright, it was obvious that people were more important to Royce Burton than money.

With that stunning realization, the protective shield around Laura's heart began to crack.

If she didn't stop looking at him like that, Royce feared his chest would explode. A cool breeze brushed his upper lip, chilling the sweat beads that lined it. Breath was painful. His lungs ached. His blood ran hot in his veins.

The intimacy of the moment affected him, aroused him, annoyed him. Two people sipping chocolate at midnight, casually discussing their entwining lives just as he'd always imagined husbands and wives would do. It wasn't real, of course. Nothing was real.

Nothing except the gleam of creamy skin where the throat of her robe fell open, and the shine of eyes so luminous they glowed like stars in a midnight sky.

As if suddenly aware of his scrutiny and the eroticism of his thought, Laura blushed prettily, glanced over to focus on the napping cat in the burgundy armchair. He wondered if she'd been fooled by his pretense that Maggie's presence this evening was the first such visit.

Royce had routinely opened the basement door to invite the amiable animal into his study. He wasn't certain why he'd felt compelled to do so. Except, perhaps, to alleviate a secret loneliness made all the more intolerable by the knowledge that all Royce had ever wanted was within his grasp, yet completely out of reach.

For weeks, he'd pretended that the sight of this exquisite woman didn't make him wild inside, didn't send his pulse racing with need. This wasn't the first attractive female he'd been drawn to. He doubted she'd be the last. She was, however, the first woman in more years than he could count that evoked powerful yearnings on such a visceral level.

He told himself that it was the natural evolution of forced proximity, of the scents and sounds of femininity invading his masculine domain. Sweet perfumes wafted from her room, mingling with the delicate aroma of baby powder to form an intoxicating blend that created the ambience of family. It drew Royce like a magnet. Sometimes he lurked in the upstairs hallway just beyond view to absorb the heady smells, the tinkling laughter of mother and child as his once-sterile house evolved into a welcoming home.

It was all fake, of course. A borrowed family, a borrowed life. Still, the soft scents, the delicate laughter, the patter of tiny feet on the polished hardwood floor touched his heart and filled him with yearning. Deep down, he wished it were real.

That wish was what angered him. Self-delusion was not a trait Royce tolerated in others; he certainly wouldn't tolerate it in himself.

Laura cleared her throat, nervously plucked at a soft sash draped over her crossed thighs, the shape of which were clearly molded beneath the long robe's silken fabric. He riveted his gaze on those thighs, envisioning a hint of bare calf concealed below the far edge of his desk, and visible only in his active imagination.

"So," Laura said suddenly. "What shall we do about the gallery opening?"

He yanked his gaze upward, saw confusion in her eyes. "We will attend, as scheduled. Marta will care for the child. The matter is settled."

She paled slightly and issued the curt nod of a reprimanded employee.

He regretted his brusque tone, but it was necessary,

more to reinforce their business relationship in his own mind. "I will, of course, supply you with attire appropriate to the occasion."

She yanked her gaze back to stare at him with obvious astonishment. "I may not be wealthy, but I do have clothes."

"Yes, yes, of course." He swallowed hard, vaguely noting a slight shadow lurking outside the study door. "However, I understand that your selection of evening wear is somewhat limited, and I presumed that you might require—"

"You've been in my closet?" Bolting upright, she clutched the chair arms so tightly her knuckles whitened. "You've actually had the gall to paw through my things, to see if I own garments meeting your social expectations?"

"Of course not. That would be most improper." Feeling strangled, he reached up to loosen his collar, and was chagrined to find it already unbuttoned and hanging limp at his throat. "I simply suggested Marta review your wardrobe so that any inadequacies could be properly resolved."

"Inadequacies?" She practically sputtered the word, but Royce barely noticed.

His horrified gaze was riveted on two bright little eyes peering around the doorjamb. A separate shadow scampered past, melting into the darkness.

Kittens. In the hallway.

He must have left the basement door ajar.

Royce stood quickly enough to spin his swivel chair into the wall just as the whiskered face disappeared into the shadows. "While you're considering the offer, I'll just, ah, take care of a personal matter."

Hoping he didn't look as desperate as he felt, he

flashed a smile, dashed out of the study and shut the door behind him.

Squinting, he bent over to peer behind a large potted palm. Two luminous eyes peered back. "Shh," he whispered, reaching slowly toward the hiding kitten. "You're not supposed to be—"

A flash of gray-and-white fur shot between his feet, and disappeared into the foyer.

"Here," he finished lamely.

Frantic, he hit a light switch, swiveling his head side to side until a swish of movement caught his attention. A tiny black tail no longer than his pinky finger flicked from the doorway of the south-wing powder room.

Royce crouched, inching forward until the vibrating fur appendage was mere inches from his flexing fingers. He dove.

The kitten leapt straight up.

Something furry brushed Royce's palm. He grabbed it. "Aha!" A flash, a pounce and a dozen needle-sharp claws suddenly dug into his spine.

Royce bellowed and rolled over.

The kitten squeaked, performed a clever midair pirouette and hit the ground running.

Gasping for breath, Royce found himself flat on his back, half-smothered when the fistful of captured fur he dragged forward turned out to be a shag throw rug. He thrashed out from under the furry carpet, grunted as his head hit the wall, cursed when his shin struck the vanity, eventually flipped onto his stomach facing the open doorway.

Battered and bedraggled, he pushed with his knees, pulled with his elbows and bellied forward, mumbling. As soon as he'd slithered through the open doorway, his forehead touched fur. Not fuzzy kitten fluff, either. Real, honest-to-goodness, grown-up cat fur.

A frisson of fear slipped down his spine as he looked up into a pair of blinking yellow eyes.

There, seated neatly on her fat orange haunches, Maggie studied Royce with the usual bemusement displayed by a superior feline when observing the clumsy antics of a human.

To his horror, a pair of slippered feet were planted directly behind the mama cat. A swish of silken fabric swirled around a pair of shapely calves as trim and enticing as he'd imagined them.

Slowly, painfully, he raised his gaze until Laura's stunned expression came into focus. He attempted a smile. It made his cheeks ache. "I don't suppose anything I say could salvage my dignity at this point."

She closed her mouth, swallowed hard and slowly shook her head.

"I didn't think so." Flinching, he pushed himself upright, rising on his knees like a disheartened prairie dog. "There's a perfectly good explanation for this."

Laura licked her lips. "I'd love to hear it."

"Yes, well— There!" Scowling, he stabbed an accusatory finger toward a tiny whiskered creature scurrying toward the stairs. "You see? They are everywhere." He struggled to his feet, puffing his chest with righteous indignation. "Your animals have invaded my home."

"Have they, now?" Much to his dismay, she didn't even try to suppress her amused grin.

"I fail to see the humor."

"I can imagine." Her gaze traveled the length of him with deliberate impudence. "A glance in the mirror may remedy that."

"Hmm?" Frowning, he leaned his upper torso back through the powder-room doorway and turned on the vanity light. To his horror, a disheveled mess of a man stared back.

The seam of his left sleeve was ripped and half his shirt buttons had popped off, exposing an indecent length of bare chest. Mauve tufts from the shaggy throw rug stuck to a stiff tousle of hair that looked as if it had been moussed with egg whites and beaten with a wire whisk.

He was, in a word, pathetic.

Humiliated, he plucked a few fuzzy pink clumps out of his hair before facing her with a defeated sigh. "I'll give you a hundred million dollars if you promise never to divulge to a living soul what you've witnessed here tonight."

To her credit, she fought her curving lips into submission. Her eyes, however, still sparkled with delight. "Do you have a hundred million dollars?"

"I'll make payments." He pushed past her, grumbling, and swooped down to claim a scampering ball of gray-and-white fluff. Holding the kitten up to his own eye level, he recognized Rascal, the troublemaker he'd rescued from behind the now-shredded wine rack. "First you instigate the destruction of my cellar, now you lead a rebellion against me."

Rascal mewed.

"No mercy this time, you whiskered wretch. You are banished to the dark place forever— Ouch!"

The wriggling kitten dug in his claws, sprang free when Royce loosened his grip.

Laura stepped forward to cradle his hand in her palms. "Oh, goodness. You're bleeding."

"Of course I'm bleeding," Royce growled. "I've been attacked."

She chuckled. "It's a kitten scratch. You'll live."

Suddenly, the entire foyer was alive with dashing, scampering, springing little animals. The black one called Cary Grant sprinted from the shadows to pounce on its calico sibling; a cottony-white Bunny-Cat zipped past the partially open basement door to squeeze beneath the apron of an antique sideboard.

Sam, the orange-and-white tabby, climbed the hat rack as if it were a convenient tree, while Rascal skidded across the polished marble floor with less than Olympian grace.

"Oh, heavens!" Laura dropped Royce's hand, plucked the orange kitten off its mahogany perch and unceremoniously handed it off like a tiny football.

"Wait...!" Royce juggled the kitten, relieved that it appeared less bloodthirsty than its aptly named brother. "What shall I do with it?" Spotting the open basement door, he cupped the diminutive feline in his palms and rushed forward just as Laura dove to capture a scurrying Cary Grant.

Royce dodged right, then left, then right again, until the toe of one shoe tangled with the heel of the other, and he found himself flat on his face, holding the orange kitten over his head to avoid crushing it.

Before he could so much as refill his deflated lungs, Laura let out a yelp and collapsed on top of him.

In the chaos that followed, Laura's watch hooked the torn shoulder seam of his shirt. She gave it a determined yank, then rolled off of his back. The sleeve went with her.

"Oh!" Propping herself up on one elbow, Laura ripped the tattered hunk of formerly elegant fabric from her watchband, holding it out as if it were a limp snake. "I'm...so...sorry."

Her gaze rose slightly, her eyes widened in shock at the same moment the delicate patter of baby cat paws traced a path along the back of Royce's scalp, then down his forehead to use his nose as a springboard. The jet-black kitten angled an apologetic glance before disappearing into the shadows.

Too dumbfounded to move, Royce lay on his belly sprawled like a prostrate monk at prayers, with one bare arm and one clothed one stretched out as if offering the kitten cupped in his palms to some pathetic pagan cat god.

This was without doubt the most humiliating, degrading, embarrassing moment of his entire life. His only saving grace was that the ludicrous situation couldn't possibly get any worse.

Or so he thought.

Chapter Six

The implacable, unshakable, unreadable facade behind which Royce Burton had shielded his true self suddenly shattered beneath Laura's stunned gaze. She was clearly bewildered, baffled by unexpected decency from a man usually in control of his environment to one now engulfed by chaos.

Royce's lips slackened and his jaw drooped, his golden gaze stripped of its wary veil to reveal with endearing clarity the vulnerability he so scrupulously concealed from the world.

Laura was touched by the transformation, intrigued by it, although the absurdity of their precarious situation did not escape her notice. Nor did the intimacy of being sprawled on the foyer floor surrounded by scampering kittens, with her clothing immodestly disheveled and his ripped into tatters.

The only creature displaying even a modicum of dignity and control was Maggie. The mama cat sauntered over to regard the flattened humans with something akin to pity.

Ignoring Laura, Maggie focused attention on the man who was now lying on his stomach, gasping, with Sam clasped in his upraised hands. The kitten leapt down and scampered away as Royce flopped onto his back and gulped air.

Maggie issued a throaty mew that Laura interpreted as a concerned query.

Royce rolled his head to one side, spoke between breaths as if the placid mama cat was one of his subordinates. "We agreed…that kitten control…is your responsibility."

Maggie meowed.

"Don't just sit there." He grumbled, sucked a breath. "Do something."

The mama cat blinked, glanced around and issued a soft roil from deep in her throat.

To Laura's amazement, all five kittens appeared like magic. Maggie strolled over to gather the nearest baby in her mouth and carried it into the basement.

One by one the rest of her brood followed, happily prancing through the open door and down the basement stairs.

When the entire feline family had retreated back to their allowable living area, Laura expelled her breath all at once. "So, how long has Maggie been on your payroll?"

"Very amusing." Royce rolled onto his side, exposing the full length of a muscular and very masculine arm. All that remained of his left sleeve was the cuff, which dangled foolishly at his wrist like a frayed cloth bracelet. "I hope you enjoyed watching me make an imbecile out of myself."

"Not at all," Laura lied. She slipped her gaze to the gleam of skin bared by his torn shirt, surprised by what she saw. It was the chest of an athlete, muscular and well-formed, with a tantalizing hint of abdominal ridge visible above the still-buttoned placket where the rumpled shirt was tucked into his slacks. "Under the circumstances, you conducted yourself with surprising, er, flexibility."

She couldn't seem to tear her gaze from his bare flesh. Nearly overwhelmed by the urge to touch him, she yearned to trace the slick sculpture of muscle and bone with her fingertips.

As she stared shamelessly, the rhythmic movement of his chest grew shallow, more erratic.

Only then did she realize that he was studying her with similar intensity. She noted with a surprising lack of chagrin that when she'd risen up on one elbow, the silken bodice of her hostess gown had drooped open, exposing enough cleavage to be conspicuous, although not particularly indecent.

Ordinarily instinct would have propelled her to rectify the situation. For a reason she chose not to explore, Laura made no move to do so. Instead, she moistened her lips, acutely aware of a pleasant, fluid warmth seeping through her veins.

The admiration in his gaze was erotic, exciting, infinitely arousing. It had been so long since she'd welcomed the blatant desire of a handsome man, let alone returned it. She was intoxicated by sensation, the sight of his burnished skin, tanned and gleaming with moisture, the scent of him, rich and vital and incredibly male.

The sound of each ragged breath, his and hers, vibrated deep within her, joining the pounding of her pulse and a sensual burst of heat that filled her with a longing so acute that she was ravished by the sheer power of it.

Laura saw Royce's eyes dilate and darken, revealing more profoundly than words that he liked what he saw and longed to see more. His gaze slipped the length of her, lingering on her hip, and again on a bare thigh exposed beneath her tangled skirt. The audible catch in his breath excited her beyond measure.

She wanted to explore him, to feel the pliant tremor of muscle beneath her fingertips, the pulse of aroused flesh between her palms.

In the moment their eyes met, she knew that he wanted the same thing. Flexing his bare arm, he reached toward her as if preparing to caress her cheek. He would kiss her if she allowed him to. She knew it. She felt it.

And she wanted his kiss more than she wanted her next breath.

With a contented sigh, she reflexively lifted her lips just as his gaze slipped past her. His eyes widened, his hand froze in midair.

A gasp of outrage shattered the moment.

Even before Laura spun to look over her shoulder, she knew what she'd see.

There stood Marta wearing a scandalized expression and a frumpy chintz robe, which she clasped at her throat as if it were a chastity shield.

She sputtered with indignation. "Have you no shame?"

Royce was on his feet in an instant. "I realize this must appear to be rather damning—"

"If you must flaunt your carnal pleasures, can you not do so in private?" Displaying a surprising lack of propriety, Marta first interrupted her employer, then totally ignored him as she directed the brunt of her verbal assault squarely at Laura. "What if the child had stumbled down to see this heathen behavior?"

Laura struggled into a sitting position, emulating Marta's modest gesture by clasping the throat of her own garment together.

Since her mind had gone blank, she had no response to Marta's indignant question and was guiltily grateful when the furious woman whirled on Royce, eyeing his torn attire with puckered scorn. "Look at yourself! Have you lost all sense of decency? You mother would be turning in her grave. She taught you better than this."

Laura, who'd often been the target of Marta's chastisement, wasn't surprised by the bluntness with which the woman now expressed her displeasure, but was astonished at her chutzpah in treating her employer in the dismissive manner one might display with an errant child.

Instead of issuing an immediate reprimand, Royce's response was solicitous, almost apologetic. "I assure you that the immoral activity you perceive was nothing beyond the remnants of an incident that was quite innocent, albeit absurd enough to defy description."

As he spoke, he assisted Laura to her feet without so much as a glance in her direction. Shifting in obvious discomfort, he turned pointedly away as she hastily tidied her tousled garment.

Guessing the reason for his chagrin, Laura swallowed hard and foolishly held up the swatch of ragged fabric. "I believe this is yours."

Accepting it without comment, he casually crossed his arms at the wrists, low enough that the tattered hunk of shirt concealed the fly of his pants, along with any telltale bulge announcing sexual arousal.

Marta regarded them both with blatant skepticism. ''An incident, was it? Sounded more like a war, what with the floors pounding and the walls vibrating.'' Her gaze dropped to Royce's bare arm and the crisscross of welts forming just below the elbow, then angled an accusatory look over her shoulder.

Laura felt the flush crawl up her cheeks. Obviously Marta believed she had ripped Royce's clothes off in a fit of uncontrolled passion, raking his skin with her fingernails in the process. Which was exactly what she'd been considering before Marta's unexpected intrusion.

''Mr. Burton was attempting to retrieve the kittens.'' Laura's stammered explanation sounded lame, even to her.

Marta raised a brow. ''Kittens?''

''They got loose, you see.''

''Did they, now?''

''Yes, but the crisis has been resolved.'' Clearing her throat, Laura took two steps and neatly closed the basement door. ''I'm sorry you were disturbed.''

Narrowing her gaze, she turned to Royce. ''I told you they'd be nothing but trouble. Cat hair all over the house, and God knows what nastiness I'll have to clean up tomorrow.'' Without awaiting a reply, she refocused on his scratched arm. ''Best let me tend to those wounds. No telling what kind of germs those vicious creatures have passed along.''

''Thank you, but I'd prefer to take care of it myself.'' Still clutching the ridiculous hank of sleeve in front of him, he spun on his heel and strode rather awkwardly into the powder room.

Meanwhile, Laura sidestepped toward the stairs, and had nearly made a clean getaway when Marta whirled on her.

"I'm a widow, not a spinster," she said with sudden calm. "I know the secrets of a man's body. Don't think you can fool me with your innocent pretense. I'll not see him hurt again, not by you. Not by anyone."

Startled, Laura studied the woman more closely, and recognized genuine concern in her eyes. At that moment, she realized that Marta's anger was not based upon vanity or control, or fear of losing her own power. It was protective anger, the kind a mother displays to guard her young.

Marta obviously cared deeply about Royce, and was devoted to his safety, his happiness, his emotional well-being.

Having recognized the motive behind the menace, Laura couldn't help admiring Marta's loyalty, nor could she control her growing fascination with the man who had inspired it.

"I'm sorry." Laura swallowed hard. "I don't know what else to say."

"Say it won't happen again," Marta snapped.

Laura's gaze skittered away. She couldn't make that promise. It would happen again.

And both women knew that.

Shifting the spiral-bound report in his lap, Royce changed positions. He plucked a tuft of orange cat hair from the burgundy fabric while his executive finance committee perused documents scattered across the mahogany desk and argued about finance terms.

Leila Winters plucked a pencil from the twist of sable hair fastened at her crown, tapped the eraser on a debt-service spread sheet pockmarked with notes. ''The interest rate they're demanding will compromise first-quarter profits next year, and send stock prices down at least one and seven-eighths. Unless they adjust their proposal by a quarter of a percent, I recommend we pass on the loan and extend our current line of credit.''

Dave Henderson was already shaking his head. ''An extended credit line will reflect on our fourth-quarter financial statement, on which Marchandt plans to base his finance investment determination. A new loan won't be reflected on the books until after the first of the year.''

''Unless his entire accounting department has mush for brains, Marchandt will be well aware that our revenue stream for early next year will not meet original projections.'' Leila frowned, adjusted her glasses. ''He'll know that we're going to need a cash infusion just to maintain current operations. Unless, of course, we budget a significant layoff in the manufacturing division—''

''No layoffs,'' Royce said.

Dave and Leila exchanged a worried glance, as did the two junior members of the finance committee, who were seated on a tapestry settee beside one of the wall-size bookcases.

Dave cleared his throat. ''Unless you're willing to forego the expansion plans, we have to present a financial structure positive enough to lure a serious investor. We may have to rethink our personnel policies.''

''No.'' Royce stood, tossing the report on the corner of his desk. In the eleven years Burton Technologies had been in existence not a single employee had ever been laid off, even during the slow times when orders trickled like cold molasses and warehouses bulged with unshipped goods. "Our employees have been promised job stability in return for hard work and loyalty. They've kept their end of the bargain. We'll damn well keep ours."

The silence of his colleagues spoke volumes. Royce knew they disagreed. He didn't blame them. Each of them had been hired for their financial expertise. They were good at their jobs, the best. The advice they gave him was solid. Usually he took it. This time, he wouldn't. Promises were sacred to Royce. He'd never broken a promise. He wouldn't start now.

Turning toward the window, he stepped away from the clustered executives and gazed out into the yard. Laura was outside playing with Jamie. The sight never failed to intrigue him, to soothe him, to make him smile. She was so vivacious, so exuberant, laughing and rolling on the grass with the giggling toddler as if nothing on earth was more important than spending that moment with her child.

To Laura there wasn't anything more important. Royce had learned that much about her. He respected that, admired her immensely. Laura was a magnificent mother, nurturing and kind, gentle and loving, yet filled with a zest for life that fascinated him.

Behind him, the conference continued. Royce half listened to the conversation, although his gaze was riveted on the beautiful woman who frolicked just beyond his reach while sunlight streamed through her tawny hair like shimmering gold ribbons.

"Next week Marchandt is sending a committee from

his New York office to check out the facilities," Dave was saying. "My guess is that the point men—"

Leila cleared her throat. "Or point women."

"I stand enlightened."

"Then by all means, carry on."

"With your esteemed permission, I shall be pleased to do so."

As always, banter between Dave and Leila was pleasant, an enjoyable and teasing diversion between colleagues whose mutual respect was unquestioned. "As I was saying," Dave continued, "the point people will be doing a complete background check on the company, as well as on key executives. They'll be chatting with employees, suppliers, banking personnel—"

Royce tuned out the rest of the conversation. He stepped to the side of the window, straining to watch Laura and Jamie as they moved across the manicured lawn. The toddler had discovered something in the grass, was holding it out in his fat little hands for his mother's inspection.

Laura's expressive eyes widened; her smile broadened into a grin. Jamie was so excited he bounced in one spot, slipped and fell on his bottom. The stunned look on the child's face was utterly priceless.

Royce didn't realize that he'd laughed out loud until Dave spoke to him.

"Is there something wrong with that, Royce?"

Glancing over his shoulder, Royce saw four quizzical expressions staring back at him. "Excuse me?"

"Is there something wrong with my decision to invite the Marchandt people to the gallery opening next week? I presumed a social setting might be more conducive to—"

"No, it's fine, great idea." Actually, Royce didn't

give a moment's thought to whether the idea was great, lousy or indifferent. He was simply anxious to return his undivided attention to the joyful scene outside the window, but was disappointed to note that the yard was vacant.

At the same moment, he heard the muffled slam of the back door and realized that Laura and Jamie had probably entered the kitchen. A glance at his watch confirmed that it was nearly lunchtime, after which the toddler would probably be taken upstairs for a nap.

Royce was aware of the baby's schedule, because he made it his business to be informed of every nuance of household activity. He particularly enjoyed lurking outside the nursery while Laura read a bedtime story or sang a soft lullaby. He wished he could do so today, but knew that the finance conference would continue for most of this Saturday afternoon, possibly into the evening.

Sighing, he regretfully turned away from the window. "So let's have a look at those alternative debt-service schedules."

The meeting droned on. Disputes were professionally aired, some decisions made while others were tabled for later discussion. Perhaps an hour after Royce had observed Laura and Jamie playing in the yard, he was vaguely aware of a thumping in the foyer just outside the study.

Engrossed in analyzing production costs, he paid little attention to the rhythmic patter. There were all kinds of noises in the house now that Laura and Jamie had moved in. Bumps upstairs, whispers in the hallway, the sound of footsteps on the stairs.

For the most part, Royce enjoyed the sounds of life

surrounding him, although he was gifted with an ability to ignore extraneous noise while preoccupied with business, as he was now. "So if we can shift production lines, we can take advantage of economies of scale to lower the per-unit cost without substantially altering the—"

"Daddy, Daddy!" The study door, which had been left ajar, suddenly burst open. Jamie rushed in, squealing happily. The toddler grinned, giggled and hooked a finger in his mouth. He was obviously pleased with himself.

He was also naked from the waist down.

Dave Henderson blinked as if hallucinating. Leila covered her smile but couldn't disguise the amused sparkle in her eyes. The two junior executives simply gaped at the cavorting toddler, as if fearing any expression at all would be grounds for instant dismissal.

Grinning madly, Jamie clasped fat hands over his bare tummy. "Me go potty all by myself!"

Royce managed to peel his tongue off the roof of his mouth. "That's, er, commendable."

"Quite commendable," the first junior executive agreed.

"Exceptionally commendable," the second junior executive chimed.

"Not to mention drafty," Leila added with a wry chuckle. "This reminds me of the time my niece interrupted a dinner party with my sister's husband's boss—"

"Jamie? Jamie!" Laura practically dove into the room, scooped up the baby, her eyes wild with embarrassment. "I'm so sorry. I just left the powder room for a moment, and—"

"Me go potty!" Jamie crowed happily. "All by my-self!"

"Ah…yes, yes, you did. What a big boy you are." Laura was red as a tomato.

Royce was certain he'd never seen a more beautiful woman in his entire life. "Laura, I believe you've met Dave Henderson, our chief financial officer."

"Of course." Despite her embarrassment and the fact that everyone in the room was privy to the business nature of their marital arrangement, Laura slipped smoothly into the social graces without missing a beat. "It's so nice to see you again, Mr. Henderson. Dotty and I had such a delightful chat at the library bazaar last week. Please give your lovely wife my regards."

"I will indeed," Dave replied with a gentlemanly nod.

"Leila Winters, our financial services manager."

Leila stepped forward, extending her hand. "I'm happy to meet you, Mrs. Burton."

"Please, call me Laura." Shifting Jamie on her hip, she stepped forward to accept the woman's handshake. "Royce speaks so highly of you, I feel as if we've already met. Is your mother feeling better now? I understand she was under the weather last week."

Clearly pleased by the personal acknowledgment, Leila beamed. "She's feeling much better, thank you. I'll tell her you inquired."

"Please do. I look forward to meeting her." Turning smoothly, she favored the first junior executive with a perfect hostess smile. "Ms. Pearson, I presume. I'm so pleased to meet you. Tell me, have you and your fiancé set a date for the wedding yet?"

Flustered but obviously pleased, Ms. Pearson lost her

executive composure only for a moment. "Next spring, mid-April. We're still at the planning stage."

Royce didn't even know the competent first junior executive had a fiancé. Obviously, Laura had done her homework extremely well and had made it her business to know enough about the company's key personnel to play her role as the boss's wife to utter perfection.

"Royce and I are so looking forward to attending," Laura said with astounding candor. "Do let us know as soon as the date has been set."

After the blushing first junior executive stammered assurance that notification would certainly be forthcoming, Laura favored the second junior executive with her undivided attention. With utmost sincerity, she congratulated him on a poetry award that Royce had never heard about, inquired about his sister's pregnancy—also news to Royce, since he wasn't aware the shy young man in question even had a sister—and wished his softball team luck in pursuing the league championship.

Within a matter of moments, exhibiting exquisite grace and superb social skills, Laura Mitchell Michaels Burton had dazzled every person in the room.

And she completed this gargantuan task while wearing a pair of grass-stained shorts and a Tweety Bird T-shirt, and balancing a half-naked toddler in the crook of her arm.

She was, in a word, incredible.

Beyond her obvious beauty and charm, Laura had another quality, one that a shrewd businessman like Royce could not dismiss. In the shadowy world of corporate politics, instinctively understanding the human psyche was every bit as important as product knowledge, manufacturing quality and having a financial fin-

ger on the pulse of international market trends. In a
competitive field, the difference between a successful,
multimillion-dollar contract or collapse into financial
ruin often came down to a single factor: establishing a
personal relationship.

Laura did that automatically. She possessed a rare
capacity to captivate, to charm, to convey an aura of
such sincerity as to convince all in her presence that
each was most important.

A rare find indeed, Royce decided, one that could
become a most valuable asset for Burton Technologies.
The pesky fact that Laura considered their alliance to
be temporary didn't faze him. Everyone had a price,
after all, especially a woman like Laura.

Royce simply had no idea how high that price
would be, or what it would ultimately cost him.

Laura could have just died.

"Me big boy!" Jamie announced as his mother carried him out of the study and hurried upstairs.

"Big boys dress themselves before leaving the wash-
room," Laura mumbled. "We'll have to work on
that."

Jamie grinned. "Want cookie."

"In a minute, sweetums. First we have to get you
dressed and—" Laura jerked to a stop as Marta exited
the upstairs guest room. "What are you doing in my
bedroom?"

Marta regarded her with no interest, then settled her
gaze on Jamie. "Do you always allow your child to
run around naked?"

"Don't worry about it," Laura snapped. "He's litter
trained."

The frumpy housekeeper squinted as if eyeing an

unpleasant bug. "I've just hung a few perks of your position in your closet. I trust they will meet with your approval."

Laura had no clue what she was talking about, and said so.

"Gowns," Marta said succinctly.

"Gowns?"

"It's nice to have a generous husband, isn't it?" A snort conveyed her disgust. "I'm sure that jewels and fancy furs are on the way as we speak."

Annoyed by her contemptuous tone, Laura put Jamie down and went to see for herself. To her shock, she discovered two incredibly elegant designer gowns hanging in her closet. One was a floor-length sheath of obsidian satin, the other was a cocktail dress sparkling with emerald sequins. "I didn't order these."

"Of course you didn't. A whispered wish is all it takes. But then, your kind knows such things."

Furious, Laura whirled around. "Return them at once."

"Excuse me?" Marta's smug smile flattened as Laura yanked the gowns from the closet and flung them on the bed. "But what shall I tell Mr. Burton?"

"Tell him that I'm quite capable of providing my own wardrobe for this tawdry little production, and I'm not so pathetic as to require costuming by a man who is clearly used to dressing his women in a style to which he has become accustomed."

Marta paled three shades.

Ignoring the shaken housekeeper, Laura scooped up her son and went into the nursery, fuming. She still had some pride left. Not much, but enough that she wasn't willing to be draped and strutted around to puff some arrogant millionaire's male ego.

It took a moment for her anger to dissipate enough to realize that strutting and puffing was exactly what she'd been hired to do.

Chapter Seven

Laura hadn't been this nervous since her high school prom. Then she had entered a balloon-bedecked gymnasium wearing a cotton church frock while her female classmates flaunted flowing formal gowns of satin and silk and frothy chiffon.

Now, as Royce chivalrously checked her plain cloth wrap at the cloakroom, Laura stood in the foyer of a gallery awash with color, glimmering with glitter, a collage of wealth and beauty that awakened memories of her own deprived youth when she'd felt like a frumpy duckling in a sea of elegant swans.

The scent of subtle extravagance announced Royce's presence beside her. He scanned the room without interest, then his gaze settled on her. "You really do look quite lovely," he said kindly. "White satin and black crepe make a statement of elegant simplicity."

Laura managed not to wince. The faux satin blouse

was a nothing more than a shiny blend of inexpensive polyester and rayon, and she'd borrowed the ankle-length skirt from Wendy, along with the fake pearl choker and matching earrings.

"This is all my fault," she murmured, chagrined by a gallery bristling with tuxedo-clad gentlemen. "Just because I stick out like a corn husk in a bushel of wheat doesn't mean you have to share my embarrassment."

His chuckle was soft, sensually intimate. "The tux felt a bit snug, that's all. Perhaps I've put on weight."

If he had, the pounds had certainly arranged themselves in all the right places. He looked smashing.

Nonetheless, Laura wasn't fooled by his courtly denial. When she'd presented herself this evening, Royce had been dressed to the nines in an Armani tux so incredibly lush that the mere sight of him had taken her breath away.

He'd regarded her attire for a moment, then excused himself. The moment he'd reappeared wearing a handsome but considerably less-formal charcoal business suit she'd realized what she had done by having refused his offer to provide her with a suitable gown.

Indignation had fueled that refusal, along with resentment that her privacy had been invaded and embarrassment that her current wardrobe was as unfashionably sparse as the hand-me-downs she'd worn as a child.

But she wasn't a child anymore. She was a grown woman, a woman whose decisions affected lives beyond her own.

Laura was proud and she was stubborn, but she was hardly a social neophyte. While married to Donald, she'd been expected to mingle with the elite and had possessed a closet full of elegance. Of course none of the gowns, furs or jewelry had actually belonged to her. It had merely been on loan to reflect the wealth and importance of the family she represented.

After the divorce, she'd owned little more than the clothes on her back and a bag of baby supplies.

"I'm sorry," Laura murmured, painfully aware that they were already being subjected to a plethora of surprised glances and stunned stares. "I've embarrassed you."

"Not at all."

"I should have swallowed my pride and allowed you to provide me with attire appropriate to the occasion."

"You are my wife. Whatever you wear *is* appropriate to the occasion. The rest of the room is simply overdressed." His hand settled in the small of her back, a gesture of warmth that should have encouraged her but only made her more miserable.

Laura had spent a lifetime emotionally arming herself against ridicule, derision, criticism and complaint. Royce's kindness and his gentle understanding unraveled her defenses. She felt exposed, vulnerable. Her frantic gaze darted, settled on a sedate private telephone situated on the gallery's service desk.

"Would you like to call the house and check on Jamie? It has been at least fifteen minutes since we left him in Mrs. Wilhelm's care, a virtual eternity to a concerned mother."

"Hmm?" Laura's head snapped around in time to see the amused sparkle in Royce's eyes. "Are you suggesting that I'm overprotective?"

"Aren't you?" His smile melded into a chuckle. "Mrs. Wilhelm comes highly recommended."

"I know she does. I—" Laura coughed away a sudden dryness in her throat. "I appreciate your efforts in locating someone with her child-care credentials."

"I'm glad you're pleased," he replied cheerfully. "Of course, Marta may never speak to me again."

That came as a surprise. "I thought Marta would be relieved that she wasn't expected to baby-sit."

"What led you to that conclusion?"

"Gee, I'm not sure. Perhaps the statement 'Don't expect me to follow that child around spoiling him rotten and catering to his every whim' offered a clue." Which was, in retrospect, rather inaccurate, since Marta did indeed follow Jamie around catering to his every whim. She merely grumbled as she did so.

Royce's smile broadened. "Marta's candor is part of her charm."

"Charm?" Laura laughed, feeling more at ease by the moment, although she wasn't certain why. "Is that what they call cantankerous belligerence nowadays?"

Royce angled an evil grin. "She's only cantankerous around people she likes."

"Oh, come on!" To her horror, Laura giggled, actually giggled, and gave Royce a playful swat on his upper arm. "There is no way on earth you can say that bad-tempered woman likes me. She treats me as if I was something smelly she stepped on in the park."

At the sound of her laughter, Royce's eyes warmed, glowing softly. "You seem to be feeling a bit more relaxed now."

It was then Laura realized Royce had initiated the intimate banter, not only to make her feel more at ease, but because he was aware that their personal interaction would be under constant scrutiny. A quick glance around the room confirmed that a substantial portion

of the glittering throng was watching them with unabashed curiosity.

Royce leaned slightly, his breath warm against her
cheek. "You do understand that in public, we must
conduct ourselves with a certain amount of familiarity
and affection."

She flushed. "Of course."

"Then prepare yourself, my dear." Royce brushed
her cheek with a kiss so delicately sensual that her
knees weakened, then slipped his arm around her waist
and ushered her into the sparkling, jeweled crowd.

"Thank you so much, Mrs. Burton." The blue-
haired woman with diamonds encircling nearly all of
her veined fingers grasped Laura's hand as if it were a
lifeline. "When the daffodils bloom outside the library
next spring, the Gardening Society will erect a magnificent plaque crediting your generous donation."

"You are very welcome, Mrs. Peabody. The people
of Mill Creek cherish the beauty your fine organization
brings to our town."

Smiling so stiffly that her cheeks ached, Laura took
a half step to the side and focused her attention on a
grinning older man and the matronly woman clutching
his arm. Both were vaguely familiar, although she
couldn't recall where they had met before. She'd met
so many people over the past few weeks that the names
and faces were all blurred together.

"How nice to see you again," she said to the
vaguely familiar couple. "Are you enjoying the exhib-
its?"

"Ah, the Wellington sculptures are magnificent,"
the man replied, his bulging belly straining against a
wine-colored cummerbund. "Georgia and I have our

eye on a particularly lithe piece to enhance our music room.''

''An excellent selection.'' Laura had barely moved a half-dozen steps inside the gallery before she'd been surrounded by patrons anxious for attention. She hadn't seen the exhibit in question, couldn't have described a Wellington sculpture if her life had depended upon it.

Since the fellow in the tight tuxedo seemed to require validation of his choice, Laura was happy to oblige. ''Only a true connoisseur would recognize the subtle majesty of Wellington's genius. I commend your artistic insight.''

The older man beamed, his flushing wife giggled, and in the space of a heartbeat, a new group had stepped in front of Laura, hands extended, eyes begging for recognition. She favored them with her undivided attention, smiling, nodding and feigning delight with even the weakest proffered witticism. Through it all, she never lost sight of the pained reality that it was her husband's philanthropic nature and seemingly bottomless checkbook, not her own sparkling personality, that drew these people like flies to a honeydew.

Royce's generosity had funded this gallery, just as it had subsidized the town library and provided college scholarships for dozens of deserving young people.

Over the past few weeks, she had learned that about him. And she'd learned so much more.

As if by magic, a soothing warmth spread down her spine. A breath later, Royce cupped his palm on her shoulder.

He drew her close, his fingertips stroking her upper arm. After a few moments of casual conversation with those clustered around them, he said, ''Darling, please forgive me for interrupting, but there are some people who are anxious to meet you.''

Royce tucked her hand beneath the crook of his arm, covered it with his own palm and guided her through the milling crowd in the gallery's main exhibit hall. The scent of him surrounded her, his strength seeped into her bones.

''You are the talk of the party,'' he whispered from the side of his mouth while smiling at those who greeted them as they passed. ''Everyone is utterly enamored of your charm.''

''How kind of you to say so.'' Laura paused to acknowledge the greeting from an unfamiliar gentleman with a smiling nod, then hesitated beside an etched bronze plaque beside the hallway toward which Royce was leading her. She read it aloud. '' 'In loving memory of Joyce Leeds Burton, whose love of beauty inspired its creation.' ''

Beside her, Royce stiffened silently. ''Marchandt's financial advisers are in the bronze exhibit hall, waiting to meet you. I'm certain there's no need to reiterate the importance of maintaining their good will.''

Clasping his fingers more firmly around the hand tucked beneath his elbow, he urged her forward, down a wide hallway dotted by intricately framed oil paintings.

Laura recalled the watercolors in Royce's study that were signed with the unique four-leaf-clover design along with the initials J.L.B.

'' 'Joyce Leeds Burton,' '' Laura repeated. ''She was your mother, wasn't she?''

''Yes.'' He nodded at a bald man balancing a glass of champagne in one hand and a plate of hors d'oeuvres in the other.

"Was she an artist?"

"She might have been, if she hadn't been forced into a life of drudgery to put food on the table."

As Royce guided her past a display of peculiar abstract bronze structures, Laura noticed the man in the tight cummerbund handing what appeared to be a check to one of the gallery attendants. When he saw her, he gestured toward a particularly garish piece and flashed her a satisfied smile.

Laura widened her eyes as if dazzled by his exquisite taste, causing him to puff his chest so proudly she feared the overextended cummerbund might split on the spot.

When able to return her attention to Royce, she spoke quietly, cautiously. "I wish I had known your mother. I'm certain she must have been a very special woman."

"She was." A sudden sadness in his eyes touched her. "My mother loved the finer things in life. Art, music, literature. It has always struck me as cruelly ironic that by the time I was able to supply the things that gave her such joy, she was no longer around to receive them."

An ache twisted inside Laura's chest, radiating outward with exquisite pain. She'd never seen so deeply inside of him before, never been allowed to view the raw emotion that still haunted him. His mother's death was a loss he would grieve for the rest of his life.

As quickly as the revelation had been made, all trace of it disappeared beneath the all-too-familiar professional veneer. A wary veil dropped over his eyes, and although his lips curved with welcome, he exuded the cautious aura of a well-armed gladiator greeting a pride of hungry lions.

Laura knew without looking that they were approaching the Marchandt delegation. She squared her shoulders, ran her tongue over her teeth and moistened her lips into a dewy hostess smile.

It was show time.

An hour later, after hands had been shaken and polite platitudes uttered, the Marchandt delegation strode past the few remaining gallery visitors and disappeared into the main exhibit hall. The crowd had thinned considerably, with gallery attendants now outnumbering clients and a refreshment table that appeared to have been picked over by vultures.

Laura studied an abstract bronze sculpture that resembled a sheet flapping on a vertical clothesline.

Royce joined her. "It's a Wellington."

"Yes."

"Quite hideous, actually."

She smiled. "Art, like beauty, is in the eye of the beholder."

He shrugged, glanced around. "One can insist that *Eau de Skunk* is perfume, but it still stinks." Creases of tension radiated from the corners of his eyes, and taut lines bracketed his mouth. "You were not impressed by the Marchandt delegation."

The statement startled her. "They were quite courteous and polite."

"As were you." The succinct observation was issued in a complimentary fashion, but held an undercurrent of disapproval. "In the future, however, I'd appreciate your effort to maintain a dispassionate expression when business matters are conducted in your presence."

Laura could have played the wide-eyed innocent at

this point, pretending that the discussion of job consolidation and transfer of manufacturing operations to overseas facilities had gone right over her fluffy little female head. Instead, she met his gaze directly. "I cannot believe that you would consider entering into an unholy alliance with an organization that refers to human beings as 'product,' and the destruction of lives as 'collateral consequence.'"

To his credit, his gaze never wavered. "It's a shark-eat-shark world out there. Sooner or later, even the hungriest fish in the pond will run into something with bigger teeth. Survivors don't swim alone."

Flicking Royce's analogy aside, Laura offered one of her own. "A dolphin may find safety beside a killer whale, but only until the whale's next mealtime. Joining forces with a predator offers short-term protection at best."

"Then one must use the time between meals wisely, don't you agree?" The retort would have seemed mild enough for one listening to the conversation, but it held a subtle edge that did not escape Laura's notice.

A voice in her mind whispered that she should simply smile, agree and drop the subject. She should listen to that voice. She knew she should.

So who was controlling the words now gushing from her busy, flapping tongue? "If by 'wisely' you mean allowing a bunch of Brussels money-men to map out the economic annihilation of an entire town, no, I certainly do not agree."

Only the twitch of a muscle beneath his ear revealed that her remark had struck a chord. "Since you were obviously listening so carefully, you must also have noted that I issued no agreement to any of the proposals that were tossed out for comment this evening."

She absently smoothed the front of Wendy's crepe skirt. "I didn't hear you issue any disagreement, either."

"To disagree at this point would have simply shut down communications, put them on notice that I was unwilling to consider certain options that I may have to use later as a negotiating tool. Divulging one's position too soon gives the opponent an advantage."

Laura was suddenly exhausted. "I know, I know. It's all a game, with players making backroom deals using innocent people as pawns to consolidate their own power."

The bitter edge to her voice seemed to startle him. Even as she avoided his gaze, she felt him stare at her as if searching her very soul.

"Your experience with the Michaelses seems to have left quite an impression upon you," he said.

It was true, of course, although she was surprised by his perceptiveness. "As a member of the family, I was privy to their private business dealings."

"And you disapproved?"

She shrugged. "It wasn't my place to either approve or disapprove. I did, however, learn more than I wished about the elitist definition of *success*."

"And what, precisely, would that definition be?"

"Power. Control. Money. Whoever has the most, wins. It's that simple."

He considered that for a moment. "It's never that simple, Laura." Grasping her elbow, he steered her toward a glass door at the far end of the room.

A moment later, they stood on a veranda lit by squat Malibu lights. Traffic sounds filtered through the surrounding foliage, and when Royce guided her to the edge of the patio area, she saw the highway just beyond the wrought-iron railing. Across the street, a glass-and-steel structure glowed with security lights that illuminated a familiar name. It was the Burton Technologies complex.

Royce gestured toward it. "That is success. That is the sum total of what I have accomplished in this world. It is all that I am, all that I ever will be."

Shadows obscured his face, veiled his expression, but not the telltale emotion in his voice. "What you've achieved is admirable, Royce. It's an extension of your talent, of your dreams, but it is not you, nor is it the measure of your worth as a human being. People are much more complex than that."

The moment he turned toward her, allowing a thin spray of amber illumination from a nearby streetlight to reveal his expression, she saw that she had fallen right into his trap.

"So you agree," he said affably, "that nothing is quite as simple as it seems."

She wasn't willing to concede that, not yet. "Success isn't something measurable in dollars and cents. The most successful people I know aren't wealthy, but they are rich in other ways. Most of all they are happy."

"So you don't believe that money can buy happiness?"

"It can't."

"Yet when faced with the prospect of marrying for happiness or marrying for money, you chose money. Why?" The deadly question was posed lightly, without rancor, yet it struck a blow to her heart. He was clearly referring to her marriage to Donald Michaels, not their own sham of a marriage.

"At the time, I didn't believe I was making that choice."

"And in retrospect?"

She considered not responding, simply because it was none of his business. But his manner was so non-threatening, so sincerely quizzical that she found herself replying with a candor that surprised even herself. "In retrospect, I realize that I overlooked obvious warning signs, mistook a needy man for a vulnerable one. Perhaps my judgment was colored by the fantasy of a lifestyle that had always seemed beyond my reach."

His smile was sad, as if he understood all too well. "Riches and jewels and fancy furs. Pretty heady stuff for a young woman who'd gone to bed hungry more often than not."

"I didn't care about the jewels and fancy furs."

"But you took them, didn't you?"

Grateful for the concealing darkness, she nonetheless turned away lest his potent vision note the flush creeping along her cheeks. "I took them."

"You took them, you flaunted them and you wanted more."

"Yes."

He fell silent for a moment, shifting beside her. When she angled a glance, she saw him staring across the street as if mesmerized by the glowing neon sign that bore his name. "Why did you give it all up?"

"The price was too high."

He turned, focused on her with such intensity even the shadows couldn't hide the disdain in his gaze. "The price of selling yourself to a man you didn't love in exchange for the use of his money."

If he'd slapped her she wouldn't have been more

stunned. Too bad she couldn't dispute him. Of course, it hadn't been the material possessions she'd yearned for, or even the money itself. It was the safety and security that the Michaelses' wealth represented, along with her belief, mistaken as it turned out to be, that she would never again suffer the hunger and humiliation of poverty.

Laura heard herself speaking before she realized what she'd said. "Is that what she did to you, Royce?"

The words slipped out without conscious thought, surprising Laura and clearly stunning Royce, whose entire body vibrated as if he'd been shot.

"Who?"

"The woman who sold herself to you for money instead of love." It was a guess, but judging by the stark expression in his eyes, it had been an accurate one.

"How did you find out about Sabrina?" His voice was low, deadly.

Laura paused a beat, took a calming breath. "You just told me. Although it wasn't a stretch to figure out that somewhere in your past was a woman more interested in your checkbook than your heart." She slid him an empathetic glance. "Don't beat yourself up over it, Royce. It happens."

"You should know," he snapped.

The change in his demeanor startled her, frightened her. She tried to step back but was pinned in place for some odd reason. It took a moment to realize that he was still grasping her elbow. She steadied herself, stared straight into the twin shadows hiding his eyes. "Tolerating personal abuse is not required by my contract. You may think whatever you like about me. I will not, however, allow you to treat me disrespect-fully. Not in public, not in private. Is that understood?''

A moment ticked by, then another. The warmth fell away from her arm as he released his grasp. He turned his head slightly, enough for the glow of a streetlamp to illuminate half of his face. ''Why did you refuse my gifts?''

''G-gifts?'' She stammered the word, as stunned by its usage as she was by the abrupt change of topic. ''You mean the dresses?''

''Were they not to your liking?''

''I liked them very much. They were exquisite.''

''Then why did you refuse them?''

''Because I couldn't afford to pay for them.''

''I expected no payment.''

''I know that. However, this is a business arrange-ment, Royce, nothing more, nothing less.'' She drew in as much air as her lungs could hold, expelled it all at once. ''The truth is that I made a mistake by refusing the gowns, because I didn't realize that in doing so, I was inadvertently compromising my part of the bargain by not properly representing you in public. For that, I apologize.''

Leaning against the wrought-iron veranda rail, he ap-peared to be gazing across the street. A closer inspec-tion revealed that he was angling a sideways glance in her direction. ''You refused them because you sus-pected that acceptance would create an obligation to me beyond what had been agreed upon.''

She couldn't deny it. ''I suppose that was part of it.''

''And because you feared actually wanting some-thing, enjoying something that could be taken away from you later.''

Only when she felt the cool iron rub her palm did she realize she'd grasped the railing to steady herself. It was as if Royce Burton had peered into her very soul, read all the secrets hidden there. He seemed to understand her better than she understood herself.

He straightened suddenly. "The gowns will be returned to you. One hundred dollars a week will be deducted from your wages to pay for them."

"I can't possibly afford—"

"By the way, I'm exercising clause six, subparagraph 3(a) of our agreement, and authorizing a merit increase in the amount of one hundred dollars a week."

"I haven't earned a raise!"

"Oh, but you will," he murmured. "I hereby invoke clause ten, subparagraph 2(g), public displays of spousal affection deemed necessary to fulfill the terms and conditions so stipulated."

Before she could utter another word, Royce slipped an arm around her waist, pulled her against his chest and fitted his mouth over hers in a kiss so sweet, so earth-shattering, that her entire body trembled as if it had been set ablaze. Her knees gave way, perhaps from sheer surprise, perhaps from the shock of a moist heat exploding somewhere deep inside.

Royce simply shifted his grip to keep her from sliding to the ground like a limp noodle. He never actually broke the kiss, simply repositioned it from her lips to one corner of her mouth, nibbling softly, as if tasting exquisite wine before brushing his lips over hers on the way to test the other side with equal care.

His whisper warmed her cheek. "I presume my contractual obligations have been conducted with the proper respect."

"Not quite," she murmured, cupping her palm at the back of his neck. "Perhaps a bit more practice."

The night air was soft as cotton, sweet with jasmine coaxed into blossom by unseasonal warmth. Indian summer, his mother had called such fall heat waves. She had loved the unexpected shimmers of heat and the delightful fragrances that wafted briefly on the wind only to dissipate with the next autumn chill.

Royce opened the car door. Laura exited the vehicle, pretending not to notice the hand he extended to assist her. She avoided his gaze, as she'd done for the past hour, ever since she'd kissed him senseless on the veranda.

Or perhaps it had been he who had kissed her senseless.

All he knew, all he could remember were two people wrapped in passion, mouths tasting and probing with frantic urgency, while hands grasped and clung with frenzied desire.

Suddenly, it had ended. He didn't know why. He hadn't wanted it to end, couldn't recall which of them had pulled away first. He did, however, remember the awkward silence, broken only by the sounds of their own ragged breathing. She had stared at him with a thousand emotions fleeting through her gaze, and he had not recognized a single one.

Now he followed her up the winding walkway, a pebbled collage of concrete studded with polished river rock imported from Europe and lit with expensive foot lamps that had been hand-fashioned from fine-quality brass. Her shoulders were rigid, her stride was direct and brisk.

Once on the expansive front porch, she passed between carved granite pillars that Royce had insisted upon even though the architect considered them pretentious, and she reached for a curved door handle so highly polished that he saw her stoic expression reflected in the gleaming brass.

When she touched the shiny handle, he stepped forward, covered her hand with his, preventing her from turning the latch.

"Do you trust me?" he asked.

Her breathing shallowed. "I don't distrust you."

"But you don't trust me, either."

It took a moment before she turned to look at him. "No."

"Good. You shouldn't." Easing her hand from the door latch, he cupped her fingers between his palms. "People are not always what they seem. Motives are rarely pure, and never completely altruistic. You are wise to be wary."

She regarded him without comment.

"Our relationship has been defined as one of mutual service," he said. "Each of us needs something from the other. It is an agreeable partnership, one that will serve us well unless—" he coughed away an annoying dryness in his throat "—unless either of us redefines our arrangement without renegotiating the terms."

She continued to stare at him as if he were speaking gibberish.

"Not that our arrangement cannot be redefined, of course." He shifted his stance, felt like a fool. "In fact, as our personal, ah, needs expand and change, it may be to both of our benefits to discuss enhancement of our relationship, as currently described. I don't believe, however, that this is the appropriate moment for us to make that decision."

Her gaze never wavered. "Well, darn. So much for the suitcase of condoms I bought for just such an occasion."

"Excuse me?"

"Here I've been champing at the bit to seduce you, and you saw right through my sordid scheme. Guess I'll have to find some other way to railroad you into my bed."

"I've expressed myself badly," he said. "I'm afraid you've misunderstood."

"Have I? Well, fear not, my rich and handsome bachelor friend. Despite my reputation as a shameless, money-grubbing hussy, your virtue is safe with me."

"It's not my virtue that is in jeopardy. It's yours." Smiling, he stroked her cheek with his knuckles. "I took advantage of you tonight, and in doing so I jeopardized a relationship I have come to value greatly. Given my behavior, you have every right to believe that I wanted more from you than our, er, contract obligated you to offer."

"And you don't?"

"Well, of course I do. You are a breathtaking and desirable woman. I'm not made of steel."

The curve of a smile gleamed from her glossy lips. "Thank you for saying that. It returns at least a modicum of my feminine dignity."

He swallowed hard. She had no idea how much he wanted her.

"Do *you* trust *me?*" she asked suddenly.

The absurdity of having his own question tossed back drew a chuckle. "I haven't given it much thought—"

"Tsk-tsk, fibbing isn't nice." She smiled sweetly.

He gave in. "No, not completely."

"Good. You shouldn't." She winked. "Because you're a breathtaking, desirable man, Royce Burton, and any woman who claims she doesn't want a taste is lying through her teeth."

Stunned, Royce stood on the porch as if rooted there. Then he closed his gaping mouth, and followed her inside.

He could not believe what he saw.

Chapter Eight

"That woman is a lunatic." Mrs. Wilhelm huffed to the coat closet and retrieved her handbag with enough force to dislodge several hangers. "Mad, she is, stark raving mad."

Before Laura could shift her own evening bag from her shoulder, Marta appeared at the top of the stairs, her face white, her mouth clamped into a thin, angry line. "At least I don't torture babies."

"What?" Horrified, Laura practically sprinted to the stairs, only to find her access blocked.

Marta spared her a glance. "The child is fine," she snapped. "No thanks to that sadistic old witch."

Mrs. Wilhelm sputtered. "How dare you?" She spun like a top, shook a fat finger in Royce's stunned face. "I didn't agree to be abused, Mr. Burton. This will cost you double."

Marta snorted. "Abused? Ha!" Pushing past Laura,

the angry woman descended the stairs like an avenging angel, clutching her abdomen and shaking one fist. "I'll tell you what abuse is. Abuse is being too blasted lazy to bring a crying child a simple drink of water."

With a narrow glare and an indignant harrumph, Mrs. Wilhelm crossed her thick arms. "One never allows a child being toilet trained to drink water before bedtime. Anyone with an ounce of brains knows that."

Laura swallowed hard. Apparently she didn't possess that ounce of brains because she'd never refused her thirsty child a drink of water, not even when requested at bedtime. "This is probably my fault for not being more specific—"

"She took away Jamie's sleep bunny," Marta announced.

Now this was serious. Laura stared in horror at the frustrated sitter. "Jamie loves his sleep bunny, Mrs. Wilhelm. It comforts him."

"It's a crutch." The woman puffed her cheeks until she resembled an angry toad. "Children must learn to do without such frivolous things."

"You see?" Marta's question was posed first to Laura, then repeated to Royce, who simply stared back with the benign bewilderment of a man who was clearly clueless as to what a sleep bunny even was, let alone cognizant of the significance. Then Marta added the coup de grâce. "Then that sadistic she-wolf turned off the night-light, just pulled it right out of the socket and let that poor baby weep in terror."

Mrs. Wilhelm tossed up her hands. "Night-lights encourage poor sleep habits. The child was not frightened, for heaven's sake, he simply wanted attention."

"And you—" Marta stabbed a finger in the baby-sitter's direction ''—were being paid to give him that attention.''

''Perhaps I would have,'' Mrs. Wilhelm snapped back, ''if I could have gotten anywhere near him.''

Marta glanced away with a sniff of disdain. ''Someone had to care for the poor child. It was obvious you weren't up to the task.''

Turning to Royce, Mrs. Wilhelm continued to plead her case. ''This maniac wouldn't let me into the nursery. She just planted herself in the doorway and threatened to do me harm.''

''I made no threat,'' Marta mumbled. ''I merely offered a suggestion. I'm quite certain the object in question would have fit the orifice mentioned, and done you no harm at all.''

Laura nearly choked.

Mrs. Wilhelm turned purple. ''I told you.'' She yanked her car keys from her bag. ''The woman is insane.''

Royce blinked, then angled a slightly panicked glance at Laura, who stood on the stair landing, her mouth gaping in disbelief.

''I'll, ah, just check on Jamie,'' Laura mumbled, then dashed upstairs, swallowing a twinge of guilt at leaving the poor man to referee on his own. Voices followed, growing fainter as she hurried down the upstairs hallway, but the anger and agitation were still being expressed with acute clarity.

A moment before slipping into the nursery, Laura heard the front door slam, and presumed Mrs. Wilhelm had left. Outside a car engine roared to life. A moment later Laura saw the flash of headlights across the nursery window and heard a frantic screech of tires.

Yes, Mrs. Wilhelm was definitely gone. Permanently

gone, Laura presumed. She certainly wouldn't permit any woman who'd remove a baby's sleep bunny to care for her son again.

She tiptoed to the spiffy car bed, smiling at the night-light, neatly plugged in and glowing softly. The raggedy, well-loved sleep bunny was tucked beneath the blanket beside the slumbering child. A half-empty glass of water was on the nightstand. A rocking chair had been positioned between the bed and the open door.

Marta had taken very good care of her precious baby.

Another twinge of guilt dug into her heart, along with the sad realization that misjudging people had become an unfortunate habit of hers.

When was it, she wondered, that she had begun to see what she expected to see, rather than what was really there?

Perhaps it had started with Donald, when she'd confused a needy man for a vulnerable one. Perhaps it had begun even earlier, when she'd secretly blamed her mother for her father's abandonment, and the deprivations that had followed.

Or perhaps it was just a lack of ability to see through the superficial and read the truth of a person's heart. It didn't matter when the lapse had begun or if it had always existed as an inborn flaw. It frightened her. If she couldn't trust herself, trust her own judgment of people and of situations, she was doomed to make the same mistakes over and over again.

And her son would be destined to pay for those mistakes.

Leaning over, Laura absently adjusted the bed-clothes, straightened the beloved bunny and stroked Jamie's cool, damp face. He was so dear to her, so very precious. She brushed a few strands of moist hair from his face, allowed herself the luxury of watching him sleep for a few sweet moments before tiptoeing back into the hallway.

She left the nursery door ajar, as she always did, and hesitated at the door to her own luxurious quarters. Something seemed amiss, she realized, although it took a moment to ascertain exactly what it was.

She paused, listening. A voice filtered up the stairway, a voice deeper and more controlled than the angry tones of the arguing females. It was Royce's voice, yet there was something peculiar about it, an ominous urgency that sent a prickle of dread across her nape.

Suddenly the voice rose, sharp and demanding. "Laura!" She froze for a heartbeat, until a second command propelled her into motion. "Laura, hurry!"

She rushed downstairs, gasped at what she saw.

Royce knelt on the polished granite tile, with Marta's head cradled in his lap. The woman's face was white, contorted in agony. Her breath came in pained gasps. She clutched her chest, writhing.

Royce looked over his shoulder, terror visible in his eyes. "Call an ambulance," he said. "I think it's her heart."

The smell of hospitals always made Laura sick.

There was something too sterile about them, as if the overpowering antiseptic scent had been troweled on to conceal the stench of death.

Hovering at the doorway, she peered into the room where Royce sat beside Marta's bed. From her vantage point, she could observe the touching scene unnoticed, hear all but the softest whisper of conversation.

It was a sweet scene, Laura thought as she watched

Royce press a moist cloth to Marta's forehead. The woman's eyes fluttered open. Her thin smile was tempered by a flinch of pain.

"Gallstones," she muttered. "How embarrassingly ordinary."

Royce chuckled, laid the cloth aside. "A ruptured gallbladder makes it considerably less ordinary. You could have died." He took a water glass from the nightstand, slipped a palm beneath Marta's chin and guided the arched straw to her lips. "According to the doctor, you've probably been having these attacks for weeks, if not months. Why didn't you tell me?"

She sipped water for a moment, released the straw with a muffled gasp of pain, then turned her face away, waiting until Royce gently lowered her head to the pillow before responding. "You had enough on your mind." She paused for a shallow breath. "Besides, I thought it was indigestion. It always went away."

Smiling, Royce replaced the glass on the nightstand. He moved from the chair to seat himself gently on the edge of her mattress, brushed the woman's crinkly red hair from her face. "The good news is that the surgery went well, and the doctor expects you to make a complete recovery."

Marta took another breath, wincing with the effort. "And the bad news?"

"The damage was too extensive for laparoscopy. They had to do a full surgical procedure."

"I figured," she muttered. "It feels like I've been filleted."

"You'll have to take it easy for a few weeks."

"I can't. Too much work—"

"Shh."

The gentleness of his touch on the frightened

woman's brow affected Laura deeply. She'd never seen a man display such compassion, such sweetness.

"Your health is more important," Royce told her. "We'll muddle by."

"That's what I'm afraid of." Another shallow breath, another painful grimace. "I don't want you to think you can get along without me."

Royce gathered her hand between his palms, studying the tubes taped to her pale wrist, where the IV needle was buried in her vein. "You're indispensable, and you know it."

"Of course I know it," she murmured groggily. "I just wanted to make sure that you did."

"I do." He laid her hand gently on the bedclothes, stroked a soft circle on her forehead as her eyes fluttered shut.

As Marta drifted off to sleep, Royce continued to sit with her, adjusting the bedclothes, smoothing her hair or simply touching her hand with exquisite reverence.

Laura continued to watch from the doorway, vaguely aware that her voyeuristic intrusion was a violation of their privacy. Still, she couldn't tear her gaze away, was awed by the compassion and obvious affection being displayed by a man whose ability to shield his feelings had been honed to near perfection.

That emotion was visible now, revealed by every nuance of his gentle gaze, delicate touch. Stripped of emotional camouflage, Royce's handsome features took on an almost magical intensity. Intuitively Laura had understood that Royce possessed a heart more fragile than he wished the world to know. But she had never imagined him, or any man, for that matter, capable of such tender devotion.

Seeing it, reading the reality of his soul through the

sensitivity of his touch and the compassionate glow of his eyes, affected Laura more deeply than anything she could have imagined.

He looked up without warning, staring at Laura with a gaze that revealed only momentary surprise before the guarded veil slipped back into place. He rose quietly, crossed the room and stepped past Laura into the gleaming, sterile hallway.

"She'll sleep for a while now," he said.

"I can stay with her, if you need to get back to the office."

He slipped his hands into the pockets of the charcoal-gray slacks he'd been wearing for nearly twenty-four hours straight. The suit coat was hung over a chair in Marta's room. "Henderson knows where I am. He'll call if he needs me."

Laura watched him cross the corridor to sit on a wooden bench a few yards from the nursing station. His obvious fatigue concerned her. After the ambulance had arrived last night, Royce had accompanied it while Laura had taken Jamie over to Wendy's. By the time Laura had arrived at the hospital, Marta had already been wheeled into surgery.

"Did you get any sleep last night?"

He shrugged. Dark circles under his eyes suggested that he hadn't, although Laura had dozed off in the waiting room from time to time. It had been morning before the surgeon had emerged to report that the procedure had been a success.

Throughout the day, Laura had been in and out of the hospital, shuttling Jamie from Wendy's mobile home to the child-care center, then back to Wendy's when the center had closed. In the process, she'd stopped by the house long enough to feed the animals and change clothes.

Now it was evening again. As far as Laura knew, Royce had not strayed from Marta's side long enough to procure so much as a cup of coffee for himself.

Laura sat beside him on the bench, shifting her straw tote to the floor. "Have you had anything to eat today?"

He laid his head back against the wall, closing his eyes. "I don't remember."

"I think the hospital cafeteria is still open."

"I'm not hungry."

"You should eat."

He sighed, rubbed the back of his neck. The hint of a smile tugged one corner of his mouth. "You sound like Marta."

"I'll take that as a compliment."

One reddened eye opened to focus on her. "That's news."

Flushing, she fidgeted with a loose thread at the hem of her knit sleeve. "Marta is fiercely protective of the people she cares about. I admire that."

Royce shifted on the bench, slipped one arm along the wooden backrest and turned to face her. "She carries that protectiveness a bit far at times, but her heart is in the right place."

"Yes, I can see that it is." Laura hesitated. "She's more to you than an employee, isn't she?"

He didn't answer right away. Rather, he gazed into space as if mentally calculating a series of possible responses, and the potential result of each. "I've known her all my life," he said finally. "She was my mother's best friend."

For some odd reason, that didn't surprise Laura. As

much as she wanted more information about this private man's painful past, she intuitively realized that requesting it was more likely to close down communication than enhance it. So she waited quietly. After a few moments, her patience was rewarded.

"When I was a child, Marta lived in our apartment building, a few doors down. I can't remember a time when she wasn't around, either laughing over coffee with my mom in the kitchen, or bustling in with a casserole, or a freshly baked cake." He grew pensive, continuing to gaze into thin air as if watching a filmstrip of the past. "When my father died, my mother went back to work, and Marta cared for me after school."

"How old were you when your father died?"

"Around seven, I think. The memory is vague, but I recall hearing whispers that it was some kind of industrial accident at the plant where he worked."

"That must have been traumatic for her. And for you as well."

"I don't remember much about my father, except that my mother never got over his death."

Laura hesitated, smoothed a piece of lint from the thigh of her khaki slacks. "When did you lose your mother?"

"When I was in college." Royce blinked, pinched the bridge of his nose. "It was her heart. She'd been ill for some time, but nobody told me. Later, Marta told me my mother swore her to secrecy because she was afraid I'd drop out of college if I'd known." He angled a rueful glance. "My mother was big on education. She desperately wanted her only son to be a success in life, and believed that a college degree was crucial to that end."

"Education is very important," Laura murmured, not knowing what else to say.

"It wasn't more important than caring for my mother during her last days on earth."

"Of course it wasn't, but I understand why she'd want to spare you the pain and worry."

"I should have been told."

"Yes, you should have been told." Laura instinctively laid a comforting palm on his knee. "How did you finally learn about your mother's illness?"

"Marta telephoned me at the dorm. I hitched a ride home in time for my mother to die in my arms."

A lump wedged in Laura's throat, nearly choking her. "I'm so sorry," she managed to whisper. "That must have broken your heart."

There was no need for a response, and he offered none. Instead, he allowed his gaze to linger on her hand, still resting intimately on his knee.

Embarrassed, she withdrew and folded her hands in her lap. "Marta mentioned once that she was a widow. When did she lose her husband?"

"About ten years ago."

A quick calculation confirmed that was shortly after he'd founded Burton Technologies. "So you brought her to Mill Creek to work for you?"

Royce's smile was quick and wry. "Marta works for no one. She does, however, offer a mutual association with those who show the proper respect and are able to appreciate her skills." His smile faded, his eyes clouded with bafflement that broke Laura's heart. "I just don't understand why a woman more dear to me than life itself would jeopardize her own health rather than ask for help."

"Perhaps Marta wasn't aware how potentially serious her condition was."

He raked his fingers through his hair, his face raw with emotion he didn't even try to conceal. "She said she was afraid that I could get along without her. Can you imagine that?"

Actually, Laura could imagine it, although she'd have ripped her tongue out with hot tongs before she'd have said so. "She was probably joking."

A crease between Royce's brows confirmed that he didn't believe that for a moment. Laura hadn't really expected him to. Marta wasn't known for her sense of humor.

"She doesn't realize how much she means to me," he said finally. "A woman who nursed me through swine flu and chickenpox, who cheered my Little League team and once cold-cocked an umpire who made a bad call, a woman who has loved me and nurtured me my entire life doesn't even realize how much I care for her because I've never bothered to mention it." He paused a beat, then a soft murmur rolled from his tongue, a whisper so frail it seemed more an extension of thought than of deliberate speech. "I never told my mother I loved her, either. I always presumed that she knew, that the words were unimportant." A quizzical expression flickered in his eyes. "The words aren't unimportant, are they?"

Laura moistened her lips, managed a ragged whisper. "No, they aren't unimportant."

The impact hit him slowly, like a blade sliding between his ribs an inch at a time. His face revealed pain in layers, each guilty stab twisting his mouth, darkening his eyes, contorting his body and soul until decades of stoic dispassion skinned down to raw emotion, bloodred and throbbing like a peeled nerve.

''Royce, wait.'' Laura's hand slipped from his forearm as he stood. Without a word, he turned, walked silently down the corridor, turned the corner and disappeared from sight.

Night air circled his face, slapping him sharply with its chill. Crimson leaves swirled in the shadows, crackled beneath his strident step. Indian summer had disappeared as quickly as it had arrived. Autumn had returned with a vengeance.

Royce walked the narrow sidewalks of Mill Creek, vaguely aware of his location, yet moving absently, automatically, as if drawn by an invisible hand.

He'd never told his mother that he loved her.

The realization had been so stunning, so desperately painful that he wanted to weep.

Tears were a luxury Royce hadn't allowed himself since childhood. Men didn't cry. Men controlled themselves, kept their emotions safely leashed, hidden from a world that would exploit any weakness.

By any definition, Royce Burton was a man. A strong man, a sly man, a powerful man, a successful man.

He was also a coward, so frightened of his own secret weakness that his mother had died believing her son was more concerned about his own future than the life of the dear woman he'd loved beyond measure.

It was too bitter to contemplate, too wrenching to ignore.

A chill wind iced his spine, pushing him forward and slicing through his thin silk shirt, a cold reminder that he'd left his suit coat in Marta's hospital room. His cell phone was in the pocket. For the first time in more years than he could remember, he was completely out of touch with his world.

He was completely alone.

Pebbles crunched beneath his shoes. Streetlamps sprayed amber light along a quiet road, deserted but for the occasional vehicle breaking the midnight silence.

The night air was cold now, so cold that his feet and nose were numb. His breath was frosty, puffs of vapor in the darkness. Royce noticed all these things but dismissed them. His mind was awash in the past, pained by regret for that which was truly out of his control.

Royce passed a darkened gas station, moved beyond a small strip mall of convenience and service stores. All were closed now, the ugly asphalt parking lot was vacant.

Crossing the street, he passed the mobile home park where Wendy Wyatt lived. Another block, and he absently turned left, into a familiar driveway where his car still sat idle a few feet from where he'd climbed into the ambulance with Marta.

He mounted the expansive porch steps, strode between the pompous concrete pillars and entered the blessed warmth of his house, vaguely aware that both the porch lamp and the foyer chandelier were lit, welcoming him.

The second floor was dark, as one would expect at such a late hour. Still, he was drawn to the landing, and he climbed the stairs silently, foolishly. He needed to see Laura and Jamie, to assure himself that they were home, that they were safe and secure.

He paused in front of Laura's door and tiptoed into the nursery, smiling in relief at the rumpled lump of bedclothes and the dozing child beneath. An amber glow from the night-light illuminated the sweet face. Royce brushed a fingertip over Jamie's cheek. How soft it was, how exquisitely tender. He automatically tidied the covers, smoothing them over the sleeping child.

A prickle of gooseflesh tingled the nape of his neck, as if invisible eyes were watching. He turned, saw nothing but darkness. A sound alerted him, a muffled squeak. He followed it to Laura's quarters, and saw the door was ajar.

Because he couldn't help himself, he silently pushed the door open a crack and peeked into the darkness. A silver spray of moonlight spread across the pedestaled bed, gleaming on strands of golden hair splayed over the pillow.

His heart raced at the sight of her, a woman who had burrowed so deeply into his heart that even the acknowledgment frightened him. How different his life had been since Laura and Jamie had become a part of it. They had brought joy and laughter to a house that had been more of an office than a home.

He hovered in the doorway, his pulse racing, his palms itching to touch her. He wanted nothing more than to crawl into bed beside her, to gather her in his arms and feel the essence of her warmth seep into his bones.

Instead, he quietly closed the door, went downstairs and retreated into his study.

Maggie hopped into his lap, purring. From his half sleep, Royce felt the animal nuzzle his palm. He issued a throaty groan, shifted slightly and stroked the cat's sleek fur. "Who let you in?" he murmured. Maggie responded with a soft trill. A moment later, he felt the vague prick of claws kneading his abdomen.

A sweet scent wafted into the room, the familiar, steamy fragrance of the upstairs bathroom after Laura's morning shower. Something brushed his forehead, something moist and soft and exquisitely sweet. A swirl of darkness clamped his mind, dragging him away, forcing him to fight his way back.

Groggily, Royce forced an eye open, only to snap it shut at a blinding blast of pristine light. The enticing scent grew closer, stronger. A voice floated as if drifting on a breeze. "I'm here."

Royce tried to respond, but to his horror, he'd been struck mute. His voice no longer functioned.

Again, he forced an eyelid open, and was dazzled by an incandescent blaze. He knew she was there, so close he could reach out and touch her, but he couldn't move his arms. No matter how hard he tried, he could not coax his traitorous hands from their task of stroking the purring cat.

The wisp of a form materialized amid the blinding luster, a swish of golden hair, a sensual feminine shape. The voice floated toward him, sweet and lyrical. "Shh, it's all right."

As he squinted, he saw her more clearly. She smiled at him, her sweet face radiant, glowing. A fluid warmth pulsed through his veins, a sensation of extreme well-being.

It was a dream, of course, the heavenly meandering of a slumbering mind. Royce knew that. Still, he cherished the beauty of the moment, the fulfillment of his secret longing with the same excitement he would have experienced if this exquisite delusion had been real.

"Good morning," she whispered.

"It is now." He reached for her, felt the heat of her slender wrist in his palm. It was his dream, after all. A man had a right to control the destiny of his own fond imaginings.

Only when he heard Laura's startled gasp, felt the weight of her softness sink against his lap, tasted the honeyed moistness of her lips did his sleep-fogged brain clear enough for him to realize that it wasn't a dream at all.

Chapter Nine

Laura's lips were on fire, a moist, sizzling flame that licked every nerve in her body. She'd been kissed before. She'd even been kissed senseless before, and by the very man who was now plundering her mouth with a passion that threatened her very sanity.

At that moment, at that incredibly erotic instant in time, Royce was the center of all that ever was and all that ever would be, the core of a universe spinning at warp speed. Shards of brilliance exploded in her mind. Lightning flashes of electric energy pulsed through her blood. She was ablaze with the heat, awash with sensations too alien to identify, too intense to ignore.

Royce's arms cradled her with such gentle strength that she melted bonelessly, was enveloped by his desire. He shifted, slipped his hands beneath her hips, pivoted her on his lap as if she weighed no more than a feather and pinned her in place with an embrace that she couldn't have fought if she'd wanted to.

But she didn't want to, couldn't even fathom the thought of relinquishing her hallowed place in his arms. And in his heart.

Because Laura did own a place in his heart. She knew it, felt it with every trembling fiber of her being. At that moment, with his lips hot upon her mouth and his arms pressing her so tightly against his chest that she could feel the frantic rhythm of his heartbeat, she knew that he wanted her as desperately as she wanted him.

The kiss gentled, allowing him to swallow her soft moan of protest as he shifted away from her. She tangled her fingers in the sleek fabric of his shirt, yanking him closer.

But it was too late.

He lifted his head, blinking quizzically. "Laura?"

Breath came in one shallow gasp, then another. It took a moment for her to realize that he was stunned to see her, as stunned as if he'd mistaken her for somebody else.

The realization nearly stopped her heart.

He released her so quickly that she nearly fell off his lap, then his mouth moved, as if he was trying to speak. Nothing emerged except a thin croak. But his stunned expression spoke volumes, and sliced her like a blade.

"G-good Lord," he finally stammered.

As Laura steadied herself on the armrest of the burgundy recliner, her own heart was thudding so loudly she was certain he could hear it. "I must admit that I didn't expect a simple 'good morning' to wreak such a passionate response."

"I'm so desperately sorry," he said in a ragged whisper. "I thought you were—"

His words were cut off by a groan, although Laura had already finished the sentence in her mind. In the fog of sleep, he'd apparently thought she was somebody else. Somebody named Sabrina, perhaps.

"No harm done." Laura judiciously extricated herself from her awkward sprawl across his lap. Weak-kneed and stumbling, she managed to prop herself against the desk on which she'd earlier placed a tray containing a pot of steaming coffee, a fresh mug and tiny packets of his favorite artificial sweetener.

Grateful that his closed eyes prevented him from noting how shaken she was, Laura managed to smooth her rumpled robe and paste on a cheery smile before he finally glanced up, apologetic and clearly chagrined.

Laura was humiliated to the core. Not merely by the fact that he'd kissed her with a fever that had practically melted her toenails, but because he'd clearly believed that he'd been holding someone else in his arms.

Whoever he'd wanted, whoever had evoked such volcanic ardor in his heart, his mind and his body, it hadn't been Laura. That hurt her more than she dared to admit.

Desperate to conceal her turmoil, she forced a casual tone, spiced with a pinch of wry amusement. "No wonder Marta has always been so insistent about personally providing you with your morning coffee. You devil, you."

A neon flush rose up his throat. "You have me at a disadvantage, since I can't issue a scathing retort to your wit without making even more of a cad out of myself."

Her hands trembled a bit as she filled the mug with

steaming coffee. "I just presumed you had made the decision to—" she paused to tear open a sweetener packet and dump the contents into his coffee "—renegotiate the terms of our relationship." She gave the brew a quick swish with a spoon, noting with some satisfaction that his embarrassed flush had deepened to a rich shade of maroon. "Those were your words, were they not? At the time, of course, you didn't believe it was the 'appropriate moment' to discuss 'enhancement of our relationship as currently defined—'"

Clearly flustered, he rose from the chair and accepted the steaming mug long enough to set it aside.

Laura continued speaking with a casual aplomb despite the fact that her own pulse was racing fast enough to be frightening. "But now that I realize you simply mistook me for someone else, I can see that my initial presumption was in error."

He studied her for a moment. "You're enjoying my discomfort immensely, aren't you?"

"Oh, yes." She might as well carry this charade to the bitter end.

"This is your way of telling me that I've behaved like a pompous buffoon."

Her forced smile faded. "No, that's not my intent at all. I guess I'm just covering my own embarrassment at your expense because—" she swallowed hard, allowed her gaze to skitter away "—because I like kissing you more than I wanted to like it, and certainly more than our contract allows."

A quiet intake of breath, a pause before he exhaled. "Do you?"

Laura wouldn't allow herself to look at him. She'd said too much already, shown him a weakness that could be used as a weapon in the future just as others had done in the past. "It's to be expected, of course. Two people alone and lonely, thrust into intimate proximity for an extended period of time. You were quite correct when you cautioned against taking our agreed-upon business relationship to another level."

"Was I?" The question was issued in a flat, slightly sardonic tone. He answered it himself. "Unfortunately, all too many amicable business arrangements have been irreparably damaged when personal interests intervene."

"Exactly."

"Our mutual goals would not be well served by capitulating to, ah, temporary physical yearnings."

She managed not to flinch, and silently congratulated herself for having adopted his own ability to display dispassion in the face of internal upheaval. "I agree completely."

A feline vocalization drew Laura's attention as Maggie sauntered from behind the burgundy chair.

"So you are here," Royce said to the purring animal. "I thought I'd dreamed you, too." Maggie hopped onto the chair, meowed once, then proceeded to groom herself. He skipped a sideways glance. "I must have been more tired than I thought. I don't recall having let her in."

"You didn't." Laura shrugged, absently stroking Royce's gray suit coat, which she'd brought home from the hospital and hung over his desk chair. "I heard Maggie mewing at the basement door and thought you might enjoy her company."

He studied her. "So you really were here in the study last night?"

"Only for a moment."

Laura decided not to mention that she'd spent half

the night pacing, worrying, waiting for Royce to return home. When she'd finally heard the front door open, it had taken all her willpower not to race downstairs to greet him. Instead, she'd listened with shivering anticipation as he'd ascended the stairs, listened to his soft footfalls travel the hallway to her bedroom door.

She'd held her breath, part of her hoping that he'd enter while another more cowardly part of her feared that was exactly what he'd do. She hadn't been prepared for the stabbing disappointment she'd felt as his footsteps faded away.

That's when she'd cracked the door just wide enough to see him enter Jamie's room. From her vantage point, she'd watched him touch the sleeping child with such reverence, such wonder and awe that it had raised a lump in her throat.

Afterward, she'd returned to her bed with tears in her eyes and a surge of emotion so powerful that she was shaken to the core.

To see a man gaze upon her child with such tenderness had cracked away the final vestige of inner restraint. This was a prince among men, she'd decided. This was the man she'd waited her entire life for, a decent man, a loving man, a man whose wounded heart could not be closed against the softness of a sleeping child, or the pain of a cherished friend.

As she'd lain there, weeping silently, she thought she'd heard the squeak of her own door opening, but when she'd looked up she realized she must have simply left it ajar. She heard Royce's footsteps descending the stairs, and had followed as if beckoned by an invisible hand.

She hadn't known what she would do, or what she

would say. All she'd known is that she had to be with him, and damn the consequence.

Now she wondered what that consequence might have been if he hadn't been asleep when she found him.

Clearing her throat, she absently fiddled with the cloth sash of her robe. "I hung your suit coat over the chair last night and tried to coax Maggie off your lap so she wouldn't wake you. It was a request she chose to ignore." Actually, the irksome cat had given Laura a rather smug, eat-your-heart-out glance before curling into a comfortable ball and purring herself to sleep.

Royce's smile made Laura's heart leap. "Maggie does have a tendency to create her own rules."

"You admire that?"

"I suppose I do."

As if aware that she was the topic of discussion, Maggie glanced up from her feline toilette long enough to issue an agreeable mew.

Smiling, Royce gazed at the animal with such obvious affection that Laura was stung by jealousy. For a split second, she actually wanted to shake Maggie until her whiskers rattled, and holler "Paws off, cat, he is *mine!*"

The silliness of that impulse, the ludicrous notion that she actually envied her own beloved Maggie, made Laura giggle out loud.

Royce regarded her warily. "Admiration amuses you?"

Laura burst into a fit of uncontrollable laughter. First she'd been kissed into the throes of utter ecstasy by a man who'd groggily believed her to be an old flame, then she'd responded with such humiliating gusto that she'd practically crawled down his throat, and now she was jealous of her own cat.

What could possibly be amusing about that?

A peculiar beep startled Royce, who glanced around the room, clearly befuddled by the sound. "What on earth…?"

Wiping tears of mirth from her eyes, Laura reached into the pocket of the rumpled suit coat dangling over the chair and tossed the ringing cell phone to Royce, who caught it as if it were a hot rock.

"You'd better answer it," she said cheerfully. "I'm pretty sure it's for you."

With that, she sauntered out of the study, still giggling madly and wondering if she was the last person on earth to realize that she had completely lost her mind.

Marta stared at the breakfast tray as if it contained raw roadkill. "What on earth is this supposed to be?"

Laura responded without looking up from her study of photographs arranged on the woman's dresser. "It's supposed to be a ham-and-cheese omelet. I'm afraid it's a tad overdone."

"It looks like a stuffed Frisbee."

"The first one was too thick to fold, so I prepared another one and put them together like a sandwich." She lifted a framed picture of Royce as a young man. He looked so happy in the photograph, so openly untainted by the wary cynicism that was too frequently revealed in his gaze now. She turned the photo toward Marta. "How old was Royce here?"

Frowning, Marta shifted against the pillows to angle a glance across the spacious, tastefully decorated sleeping-and-sitting area that comprised her quarters.

"About twenty, I think." She poked the singed omelet with her fork, judiciously lifting a corner to peer inside. "You didn't try to feed one of these to Royce, did you?"

"Actually, I did. He paled slightly, but was otherwise quite polite." Sighing, Laura set the photograph back on the dresser and folded her arms. "I've never developed much of a talent for cooking, I'm afraid. Royce will be delighted when you're feeling well enough to prepare something edible for him."

The comment clearly pleased Marta, although she maintained her rigid expression. "I'm feeling well enough now."

"You had major surgery less than a week ago. The doctor only released you because we assured him we'd take good care of you."

Marta laid down her fork and issued a snort of disgust. "Maybe it tastes better than it looks."

"I can fix you something else if you'd prefer. I'm pretty good with instant oatmeal. At least, Jamie eats it."

"Jamie eats cat food."

"He does not eat cat food. He simply tasted it out of curiosity."

"He filled up a bowl with kibble and poured milk on it."

"Perhaps he presumed it was cereal."

"Or perhaps he knew this—" Marta cast a dismal glance at her withered omelet "—was the alternative."

Laura smothered a smile. True, she wasn't the world's finest chef, but she could prepare an edible meal when necessary. She'd deliberately allowed Marta's breakfast to overcook just enough for the woman to feel as if her own kitchen expertise was sorely missed. "You could be right," she told Marta. "I really don't enjoy cooking much, probably because I was responsible for preparing meals for my younger siblings when I was barely tall enough to reach the stove."

From the corner of her eye the crafty housekeeper angled a glance, looking away when she saw Laura watching her. "That's a shame." Marta busied herself sawing off a cheesy, bite-size portion. "Children ought to enjoy their childhood. Adult responsibilities come soon enough." She lifted the fork to her lips, hesitating only a moment before nibbling a small taste. "Not terrible," she opined, popping the entire bite into her mouth.

While Marta continued to consume her breakfast, Laura wandered the spacious, sunny room. A sitting area in the corner was particularly inviting, with a comfortable lounge chair beside a lamp table, on which a paperback novel had been opened and laid facedown, as if it had been set aside quickly, without benefit of a bookmark. "I wouldn't have guessed you enjoyed science fiction," Laura remarked.

"Reading is good for a body." Marta chewed, washed the bite down with a swallow of orange juice. "Fiction, nonfiction, thrillers, mysteries, romance. I like it all." The woman paused a beat. "You can read that when I'm through, if you want."

"Thank you. I'd like that." It was a small peace offering, one Laura relished. The more she learned about this complicated woman, the more she appreciated her, appreciated the nurturing and support she had so selflessly provided Royce over the years. "Royce tells me that you and his mother were friends."

The fork paused for a moment before Marta nipped

off the bite. She chewed longer than necessary, as if formulating a reply. "Joyce was a fine woman. Too gentle and naive for this world, if you ask me. Of course, the world never forgave her for that."

"Tell me about her."

Marta's gaze narrowed. "Why?"

"Because Royce is a part of her."

The older woman laid down her fork then, took the time to dab her tight mouth with a napkin. After a moment, she crushed the linen in her hand and stared across the room. "Don't set your sights on Royce Burton. You'll regret it."

The woman's candor and ominous tone surprised Laura. "That isn't a threat, I hope."

"It's a warning. Royce is a good man, but his work is his life. There's no room for a wife, a family." She paused, angled a pointed stare. "No room for a mistress, either."

Instead of flushing or looking away, Laura met her gaze directly. "So which was Sabrina?"

What little color remained in Marta's cheeks faded instantly. "What do you know about her?"

Laura managed what she hoped was a nonchalant expression. "Only what Royce has told me."

"He told you about Sabrina?"

"A little." Actually, he'd told her almost nothing, but it seemed self-defeating to let Marta know that, particularly when she was hoping to glean information. "I know that Sabrina was special to Royce, and that she broke his heart."

"Royce has a talent for getting his heart broken." Marta suddenly pushed the tray from her lap, flinching at the effort. Laura crossed the room in an instant, reaching for the tiny vial of pain pills on her nightstand.

Marta stopped her. "I don't want those."

"They'll make you feel better."

"They'll make me feel like I've got cotton in my brain." She winced again, making no protest as Laura removed the breakfast tray and set it aside. "I'm sick of being fuzz-headed, I'm sick of sleeping half the day, I'm sick of being sick."

"I know," Laura murmured, gently fluffing the woman's pillows. "You've made a remarkable recovery so far, but you can't hurry these things or you'll end up back in the hospital."

"Might as well be in the hospital, for all the good I am here."

Her woeful expression touched Laura's heart. "You are needed desperately, Marta. My lack of culinary expertise attests to that. Besides—" lowering her voice, she cast a conspiratorial glance toward the open bedroom door, assuring she wouldn't be overheard "—I was hoping you'd help me prepare supper tonight. If you're up to it, of course."

Marta's expression momentarily brightened, then faded into a scowl. "How can I do that if I'm chained to this dadgummed bed?"

"The doctor wants you to exercise by walking at least twice a day. I don't see why one of those walks can't be into the kitchen, which happens to border on the family room, along with a perfectly lovely recliner where you could be quite comfortable." Laura wiggled her eyebrows. "The fact that you could watch my cooking progress and offer tidbits of advice to keep me from poisoning the entire household would be a handsome benefit, don't you think?"

A grateful smile grooved a wreath of happy laugh

lines along her frail cheeks. "A matter of life and death, I'd say."

"At the very least." Relieved, Laura returned her gaze to the cluster of framed photographs on the dresser, settling on the photo of a younger, more vibrant Marta with a handsome older man, whom she presumed to be the woman's now-deceased husband. There was another photograph of Marta with a laughing, dark-haired woman that looked a lot like Royce. "That's Royce's mother, isn't it?"

Marta followed her glance. Her eyes softened. "Joyce and I used to spend one afternoon a month just gallery hopping and studying the Old Masters in various museums. That picture was taken on a trip upstate, to visit a showing by a young artist whose technique she found particularly fascinating." A sadness crept into her gaze. "It was our last outing together."

"Why?"

She shrugged, flinched, shifted beneath the bedclothes. "Joyce's husband died, she went back to work to support her son. There wasn't any time left for herself after that."

"Royce told me that you were like a second mother to him during his childhood."

"He said that?"

Overcome by a surge of gratitude, Laura lifted one of Marta's hands and held it lovingly between her own palms. "He said that you were always there for him, and for his mother, and that you were more dear to him than life itself."

A gleam of telltale tears brightened her eyes. Her mouth quivered with emotion. "Nonsense." She snatched a tissue and blew her nose.

"Marta—"

"Danged fool stitches itch." She grabbed another tissue and dabbed her moist eyes. "I feel like a gutted trout."

Since Marta clearly wasn't comfortable with any discussion that touched her own deeply held emotions, Laura discreetly followed her lead and changed topics. "When I was in high school, my mother had a hysterectomy. The stitches were driving her crazy, they itched so badly. A neighbor who'd been raised in Cambodia prepared a herbal salve that she found quite helpful. I think I can duplicate it, if you'd like."

The woman sniffed, shrugged, skidded a sideways glance, but didn't refuse the offer.

"There's an Asian market not far from Jamie's day care. I'll stop by on my way home this afternoon." Laura gathered the utensils and rumpled napkin and set them on the tray. "What should I pick up to prepare for dinner this evening?"

Marta plucked at the bedclothes. "It's not easy to ruin a pot roast."

"Pot roast it is." She set the tray by the bedroom door. "Has Royce mentioned the dinner party he's hosting for the Marchandt people?"

The question seemed to offend her. "Of course. We've been planning it for weeks."

"That's wonderful, because I just heard about it, and frankly, I haven't a clue how to prepare something so...extravagant." Laura had organized dozens of exquisite parties at the Michaelses' home. "There will be so many important people attending, more than we can possibly seat in the dining room." She heaved a sigh, allowed her eyes to widen as if the entire process was alien and frightening to her. "I just don't know where to start."

Marta clucked, shook her head and issued a snort that appeared to Laura as more one of relief than disdain. "That is exactly why I've prepared the menu for a European-style buffet. I contacted the caterers weeks ago. The florist is scheduled to prepare sample centerpieces, but you'd better call to confirm. Oh, and the rental service for the buffet tables, extra seating— Do you need to write this down?"

"Ah, yes, that might be a good—"

"Pencil and pad in the drawer," she muttered with an offhand gesture toward the lamp table in the sitting area.

Laura retrieved the items and scribbled madly as Marta rattled off a seemingly endless list of details.

Twenty minutes later, Marta leaned back against the pillows, her eyes shining. "You'll screw something up."

"I'll try not to."

"This is important to Royce."

"I'm aware of that."

"You'd better give me daily progress reports so I can keep an eye on things." Clearly pleased with herself and the affirmation of her authority, Marta reached for a nearby glass of water.

"All right." Laura tucked the pad of paper into her slacks' pocket. "On one condition."

Marta's hand froze in midair. "What condition?"

"Tell me about Royce's relationship with Sabrina."

Flexing her fingers, Marta withdrew her hand, folded it in her lap and fixed Laura with a thunderous glare. "That's none of your business."

"I know, but that's the deal."

"It's blackmail."

"Yes, I suppose it is." Smiling pleasantly, Laura waited.

Obviously torn, Marta scowled fiercely, one last burst of reluctance before she finally broke down. "None of this came from me, you hear?"

"I won't breathe a word."

After a pause, Marta began to speak. Slowly at first, then with increasing fervor she described a tale of grief, greed and betrayal that shocked Laura, horrified her, and finally brought tears to her eyes.

For the first time, Laura felt as if she truly understood the complicated man she had married. And she finally realized why she was falling in love with him.

Hot water sluiced over her body, steam enveloped her, filling her lungs with every breath. She reveled in the heat, holding her face up to a comforting, watery massage. The scent of herbs and lilac filled her nostrils with the sweet tang of her favorite body wash. Aromatherapy, she supposed. She loved how the fragrance clung to her body, soothed her weary mind.

Only when the water began to cool did she reluctantly turn off the shower and step out into the steamy bathroom.

It was late, nearly 11:00 p.m. She was exhausted by her added duties of cooking, cleaning and caring for Marta. That, combined with two charity functions this afternoon and keeping track of an exuberant two-year-old all evening had worn her to a frazzle.

She toweled off thoroughly, slowly, enjoying the tingling massage of terry cloth against her skin and wet scalp. To treat herself, she rubbed silky body lotion over her arms and legs, a fragrance that complimented the heady floral scent of the cleansing wash. After draping the damp towel back on the rack to dry, she shrugged on her robe and slipped out into the hall.

A light shone from beneath the master bedroom door, announcing that Royce had completed work and was preparing to retire for the evening. Laura paused a moment before returning to her own bedroom.

After closing the door, she crossed the room to rummage through a luxurious Victorian dresser, part of a magnificent bedroom suite consisting of gleaming nightstands, a classic armoire and a magnificent bed draped with exquisite silk edged with hand-worked lace that matched the room's classic window treatment.

The bedclothes were a fluffy pile of downy comforters, cashmere blankets, the finest satin sheets, and pillows so thick and soft that nuzzling into them was like kissing a cloud.

Royce had supplied the furnishings, of course, along with the extravagant tapestry armchairs, reading table and antique linen chest. The room itself was larger than the entire apartment from which she'd been evicted months ago. She'd been so stunned by the exquisite decor that she hadn't even noticed there wasn't a private bath until Royce had apologized for the lack of one.

After living with Wendy, where two adults and three children shared a facility no larger than the average closet, Laura hardly considered crossing a hall to a luxurious bath with two washbasins, a massive tub, and a separate shower facility that could accommodate a small army, to be a major inconvenience.

Rooting through a drawer containing her meager supply of sleepwear, Laura selected a slightly worn flannel gown with lace trim that was limp from repeated washing. She made a mental note to splurge on some silky nightgowns. Now that she had a regular income and the Michaelses had officially dropped the custody suit, she was finally making progress in paying off her debts, and had even managed to purchase some new togs for Jamie, who was growing so fast he needed a larger size every few months.

Laura was preparing to shrug off her robe when she glanced at her bare wrist and realized she'd left her watch on the bathroom vanity. Not bothering to retie the sash, she held the robe together and hurried into the hallway. A spray of soft illumination emanated from the bathroom, which confused her since she was fairly certain she'd turned off the light.

She hurried to the doorway and skidded to a stop, unable to believe her eyes. There was Royce, standing in the middle of the still-steamy room, clutching her damp towel to his face and inhaling the fragrance.

A gasp slipped from her lips before she could stop it.

He turned quickly, still holding the towel in his hands. His eyes were dark, intense. His lips were slightly parted. He said nothing.

He didn't have to.

Laura's heart thudded once, then began to pound so loudly that she feared he could hear it. Her pulse raced hot in her veins as he came toward her slowly, purposefully.

She moistened her lips, deliberately released the bodice of her robe, felt the humid air brush her skin as the fabric fell open.

He lowered his gaze, caressed her bare breasts with a longing look. His eyes glittered; his breath came in tortured gasps. "I want you," he whispered.

Her heart nearly burst out of her chest. "I know."

He tossed the damp towel over his shoulder and scooped her into his arms.

Laura clung to his neck, heard a soft intake of breath and realized it had come from her. "Does this mean we are renegotiating the terms of our contract?"

Royce carried her across the hall, kicked open the master suite door, laid her on his bed and seductively unbuttoned his shirt. When he reached the fastener of his slacks, Laura's gaze was riveted to the erotic bulge of his arousal.

He smiled. "Does that answer your question?"

She licked her lips, feeling as if she'd swallowed a brick. "Yes," she whispered. "It certainly does."

Chapter Ten

"No—" Laura gulped a breath "—wait."

Royce stood beside the bed vaguely illuminated by moonlight spraying through the louvered windows. At the sound of her ragged whisper, he went utterly still, his fingers still pressing the middle button of his half-open shirt.

Laura rolled over, sinking into the luxurious bed-clothes as she pushed herself upward. When she was kneeling on the bed, she reached out, laid a tremulous palm over his hand. "Let me."

For a moment he stood unmoving, as if he didn't understand her request. When he slowly lowered his hands to his side, she inhaled deeply, willing her quivering fingers to perform. To her relief, they did, delicately unfastening each button from its binding and revealing tantalizing male flesh inch by glorious inch.

Firm muscles flexed at her touch, a telltale quiver as

her fingertips brushed bare skin. When her knuckles skimmed the waistband of his slacks, she tugged the shirt from its belted prison and unfastened the final button. The fabric fell open, unfettered and free. Her palms itched to touch him, trace the contours of his strength and absorb his healing heat.

She indulged herself, sliding her open hands upward, from the ribbed muscles of his abdomen, over the rounded strength of his upper chest and finally to the curve of his shoulders. Dipping her fingers beneath the shirt, she pushed the fabric away. He shrugged off the sleeves. The garment fluttered to the floor.

Even in dim shadows the outline of his well-formed torso made her mouth water. She traced the contours of his sculpted shoulders with her palms, fluttered her knuckles along the hardened framework of his upper ribs.

"I wish I could see more," she murmured, feeling instantly stupid to realize she'd expressed the intimate thought aloud. "I mean, better. I wish I could see better." Her palms became moist; her mouth went dry. "Do you prefer darkness? I mean, some people do."

"The choice is yours," he whispered. "I'm flexible."

She could tell he was smiling, even if she couldn't see the gleam of his teeth. "What an enticing image that conjures."

Encouraged by his soft chuckle, she slid her fingertips down to brush his navel. "Of course, I have only your word for that."

He reached toward a small lamp on the nightstand. "Are you questioning my veracity?"

"Not at all. There are simply some things one wishes to test for oneself." A soft glow lit the room, illuminating the gleaming flesh her fingers so eagerly explored. She swallowed a gasp of amazement. He was truly magnificent, without a single ounce of visible fat on his entire torso. She licked her lips. "Bummer, no love handles. What am I supposed to hang on to?"

He laughed, slipped his hand beneath her nape and watched her hair flutter through his fingers. "I'm sure you'll find something interesting."

She drew a breath, danced her knuckles along the waistband of his slacks. "In that case, perhaps I'd better keep looking."

"By all means."

With a deft flick of her fingers, the fastener at the top of his zipper popped free.

"You've done this before." His voice caught just enough to reveal that he, too, was more nervous than his demeanor would indicate.

"Once or twice," she murmured, without commenting that the action had usually been performed merely to undress a drunken husband who'd passed out on the bed.

Having lowered the zipper, Laura sat back on her heels, desperate to prevent him from seeing how inadequate she felt. "We passionate temptresses are always looking for new ways to hone our craft."

"Is that so?" The question was posed quietly, without rancor. He tucked his curled fingers beneath her chin, urging her to look at him. "I don't want you to feel that you can't be honest with me."

With some effort she met his gaze. "I haven't had sex in nearly two years, and quite frankly I'm afraid I've forgotten how."

He smiled, trailed his hand from her throat to her collarbone, where it lingered a moment before he

brushed his knuckles downward along the sleeve of her
robe. "In that case—" he laced his fingers with hers,
and squeezed her hand "—this will be a refresher
course for both of us."

Grateful tears seeped into her eyes, much to her horror. In her experience, lovemaking had been more per-
functory than seductive. She'd never had a man exhibit
much regard for her feelings, let alone humble himself
to comfort her. A simple act of kindness, one that
touched her deeply.

Blinking, she turned her head away to dab the revealing moisture with her free hand. "The blind leading the blind," she murmured, hoping a humorous remark would distract from the emotional display. "Then
again, I've always heard that a knowledge of Braille is
helpful in romantic situations."

Royce would not be distracted. Instead, he knelt beside the bed so that they were face-to-face. He was
holding both of her hands now, entwining her fingers
with a reminiscent sweetness of tentative young lovers
exploring each other for the very first time. "I won't
pretend that I don't want you physically, that desire is
not pulsing through my body and my mind with a force
beyond reason. But whatever happens tonight, or
doesn't happen, it must be what is right for you. Regret
is a terrible thing. I couldn't live with myself if I caused
you to experience it, even for a moment."

She closed her eyes to compose herself. When she
opened them again, she drew both of his hands to her
lips and kissed each of the strong, masculine fingers
that were so intricately laced with her own. "I won't
regret it."

Emotion flashed through his eyes, a gleam of wonder
that touched her deeply. He closed his eyes and bowed

his head until their foreheads touched, a kiss of brows that seemed somehow more erotic than the most passionate melding of mouths.

"You are so beautiful, Laura."

A shiver of pleasure skittered down her spine. "You haven't seen all of me yet. I do have love handles."

"I adore love handles." He disentangled his fingers from hers, reluctantly she thought, and immediately caressed the sensitive flesh above her breasts with the back of his hand. A whisper of air tingled her nipples, exposed as the robe fell apart.

She rotated her shoulders, allowing the garment to slide away, then slipped her arms from the sleeves. His muted intake of breath startled her. Suddenly self-conscious, she automatically folded her arms in front of herself.

Royce hesitated only a moment, then he stood and seated himself on the mattress beside the spot on which she knelt.

"What are you doing?" she asked as he bent over, reaching toward the floor.

"Untying my shoes."

"Why?"

"Because I can't get my pants off over them."

She flushed, totally disoriented by her own stupidity. "Of course you can't. What a silly question."

Turning his head, he smiled up at her. "There are no silly questions." One shoe thumped to the side. "Only silly answers." A pull, a twist, a second thump. He stood, slipped off his slacks and tossed them over his shoulder with a wicked grin that made her laugh out loud. "I thought you might be more comfortable if both of us were, ah, defrocked."

"Wow." She eyed his royal-blue bikini-cut briefs

with a low whistle. "Who'd have guessed the seductive secrets lurking beneath that elegant Armani style."

"There's more to style than banker grays." Humming an off-key chorus of bump-and-grind music, he yanked off a sedate black sock, twirled it as if it were a silk stocking. "How am I doing?"

"Not bad, but you're certainly no Gypsy Rose Lee." She chuckled as he gave an awkward belly bump, then tossed the sock over his shoulder. "Or Gypsy Rose Leroy, as the case may be."

"I hope you know that I wouldn't make this kind of fool out of myself for just anyone."

"I'm honored."

"You should be." He hooked his thumbs in his briefs.

"No, wait." She pivoted, slipped off the bed and stood before him, nude and unashamed. "Let me."

His pupils dilated, his chest twitched, and he lowered his hands to his side. "All right."

She felt him tremble as she slipped her fingertips beneath the elastic. The briefs were distorted by his arousal, and her hands suddenly shook with anticipation. Slowly, gently, she eased the silken garment over the bulge until his flesh sprang free.

Dropping slowly to her knees, she lowered the briefs until they pooled at his ankles. He stepped out of them, then flipped them away with his toe. Self-consciousness melted away in a burst of reverence for his perfection, his maleness. She caressed his thighs, thrilled by the prickle of tiny hairs against her palms. Before she had time to consider her actions, she slipped her arms around his waist, laid her face against his belly and held him close. She felt the tremor move through him, quivering from the core of his solar plexus outward, and through his limbs.

He touched her head, brushing her hair with his fingers. "Laura..."

Whatever he'd planned to say dissipated with his next breath as she shifted to touch his erect flesh with her lips.

She cradled him between her palms, kissing him there so sweetly, with such reverence that she was amazed that an act she'd never performed before came so naturally to her.

Above her, she heard the hiss of his breath, felt the heat of desire pulse against her grasping palms. His fingers tangled in her hair, urging her closer until her forehead rested against his taut belly.

When she took him into her mouth, he groaned, slipped his hands under her arms and lifted her to her feet. "No more," he said, gasping. "It's your turn."

Before she could do more than grasp his upper arms to steady herself, he'd lowered his mouth to her breast. A moan of pleasure slipped from her lips as he suckled her gently, turning his attention from one tight nipple to the other until she thought she'd go mad from the wash of exquisite sensation. Shards of fire danced like the heat of a thousand sparklers alight throughout her body, each jolt more erotic than the last.

She clung to him, vaguely aware of squeezing his biceps with such force that she feared her fingernails might pierce his flesh, but she was helpless, her body shaking with a passion beyond her experience.

While his seeking mouth worked its magic, his hands prowled her body, exploring the curve of her back, the tuck of her hips, the sensitive flesh of her inner thigh. When his fingers found the most intimate part of her, she uttered a hoarse cry and sagged forward as her knees buckled.

He shifted, holding her up with one arm while his free hand probed sweetly, deeply, until his silky welcome was assured. A trail of moist kisses warmed her from her breast to her throat, then covered her face. His breath brushed her skin, and she vaguely realized that he was whispering. Sweet words, erotic and passionate, individually inaudible, but melding together into her mind with explosive power.

With frightening ease, he pivoted, slipped an arm beneath her thighs and lifted her into his bed. In less than a heartbeat he had joined her there, gathering her into his arms and continuing to kiss her face and lips until a blaze of colors swirled through her mind, and she was breathless with longing.

When he moved over her, she opened herself to him without fear or hesitation. It was Royce who paused, a motionless moment as he pressed himself intimately at the threshold. Supporting his weight on his elbows, his hands sought hers, cupping them gently in his larger palms. He stared deeply into her eyes, as if seeking some secret truth she had hidden there.

She wanted to speak, wanted to reassure him, but her voice caught in her throat, drowned out by her gasp of pleasure as he entered her, slowly, sensually, filling her with his power.

And she filled him with her love.

He cradled her in his arms gently, fearing that movement might wake her. She was so beautiful to him, so very special. Moonlight cast a silver glow on her face, serene in slumber, regal in repose. A strand of golden hair draped over her closed eyelid, traced the side of a slightly snubbed nose to rest at the corner of her mouth. With each rhythmic breath, her nostrils flared as she inhaled. The errant hair fluttered as she exhaled. For some reason, that fascinated him.

Royce watched for several moments before carefully lifting the strand with his fingertip and smoothing it into the tousled mass splayed across his pillow.

She snuffled softly, burrowed against him with a quiet sigh. He indulged himself, stroking a knuckle over her silken cheek, laying his fingertip against her throat just to feel the reassuring tempo of her pulse. A tiny sound slipped from her lips, a muted moan carried on a breath, the contented utterance of a satisfied lover. A frisson of delight prickled his nape. It had been a long time since he'd been so happy.

Or so scared.

Royce wasn't certain which emotion was most dominant, but they clashed like warring Titans inside his mind. For Royce, happiness was a fleeting cruelty enhancing the inevitable torment of eventual loss. Everyone he'd ever loved had left him, everyone except Marta, whom he'd nearly lost last week. Someday he'd lose her, too. Life itself is a terminal condition, a temporary journey toward the permanence of death.

Royce could deal with that. He didn't fear death, at least not his own. He feared the heartbreak, grief and loneliness of being left behind. But he'd learned to deal with that, too. Pragmatism had its rewards.

Beside him, Laura sighed in her sleep, flexed her slender fingers against his rib cage, as if assuring herself that he was still there. The proprietary gesture chilled him, perhaps because the subtle possessiveness of it seemed even more intimate than the physical coupling they'd just shared.

He gently disentangled himself, went into the spacious master bath, gleaming with opulent elegance. He turned on a row of sparkling vanity lights, opened a polished gold faucet, splashed water on his face over one of two separate washbasins carved from a single length of hand-hewn Italian marble.

The icy chill invigorated him but did little to clear the cobwebs in his mind, or cool the irreconcilable quandary of disparate emotions.

"Royce?"

Her soft call was barely audible over the rush of water, but he heard it.

She called out again. "Is something wrong?"

Every nerve in his body went on alert. He didn't know why. Turning off the water, he snatched a thick towel from a nearby rack. "Nothing's wrong." He tossed the towel aside, took a deep breath and propped himself on straight arms over the polished vanity top. "I'm sorry I woke you."

The bed squeaked. He didn't know whether fear or anticipation made his heart leap.

A moment later, she appeared in the doorway, tying the sash of her robe. She regarded him for a moment before her gaze circled the room, lingering on the hexagonal Jacuzzi tub surrounded by live ferns and tropical foliage. Her gaze paused again at the huge, glass-enclosed shower with three separate showerheads. "This is lovely. Gorgeous tile work, and I love the polished marble and decorative greenery. There are so many mirrors, the entire space seems to go on forever." She returned her attention to him with a wary smile. "It's very 'you.'"

He wanted to hold her. He really did. "What exactly is 'me' about it?"

"All of it. Like the rest of your lovely home, the decor is tastefully elegant, expansive and expensive, an irrefutable pronouncement of your personal style and success."

He couldn't argue that. "Quality and style are two criteria by which society judges us. How we live is not simply a reflection of individuality, but the result of choices we've made."

She studied him for a moment, then her lips curved into a smile that could have been sad or poignant or even disapproving. "You're wearing your armor again, I see."

That took him aback. "I don't know what you mean."

"I think you do." Moistening her lips, she reached out to take his hand. He automatically closed his fingers around hers and held on for dear life. "You're thinking about her, aren't you?"

A sudden chill slipped through him. "Who?"

"You know who." She glanced away, but not before he noted a sheen of moisture in her eyes. "I know about Sabrina, Royce. I know what she did to you."

It took a moment for his heart rhythm to normalize. He swallowed, took a breath and responded with the tone of respectful nonchalance that had always served him well. "Marta, I presume."

"Marta told me, yes. Please don't be angry with her. I, ah, insisted."

"I'm not angry with Marta."

"Are you angry with me?"

"No." He lifted her hand to his lips, kissed it gently. "I simply caution you against making judgments or taking inferences from past events that you may not fully understand."

"I'd like to understand, Royce."

"Why?"

"Because all that has happened to you has made you the man you are today. I want to understand that man, Royce. I want to understand everything about him."

"There's little to understand, really. Poor boy meets poor girl, poor girl wants rich boy, poor boy gets rich, gets girl, loses girl to richer boy. A tired old fiction plot, reworked for real life."

"That seems an oversimplification of the facts as I understand them."

"Perhaps your understanding is an embellishment of the facts."

"Perhaps." Her smile softened into one of encouragement, rather than the sympathy he'd feared. "All I know is that Sabrina was your college sweetheart and your first real love. I know that she left you for the son of a multimillionaire when you were barely out of your teens, only to reappear years later when you had become a wealthy industrialist in your own right. Is that correct so far?"

"I really don't want to discuss this, Laura."

"I also know that after she returned, you showered her with gifts, trips, money, all the extravagances that you hadn't been able to give her when you'd both been struggling young students."

Pain knifed through him at the image her words evoked, memories of Sabrina's joyous smile when her material wishes were granted, her pouting silence when they weren't. But he'd granted nearly all of her wishes because her happiness had revealed more eloquently than words that he was worthy of being loved.

Laura's scent surrounded him like loving arms as she stepped closer and caressed his bare arm. "I know that she agreed to marry you," she said softly. "And that she left you for someone else a week before the wedding."

"Someone richer." The bitter edge on his voice startled him, but he was helpless to control it. "Someone with royal blood."

Laura's eyes softened. "I know."

"It's difficult to compete with a man who rules his own country." A bark of maniacal laughter slipped out without his permission. "A woman who'd always wanted to be a princess runs off with a billionaire prince who promptly crashes his private jet into the Atlantic Ocean and kills them both. Ironic, isn't it?"

"It was a tragedy, a terrible tragedy, but it happened a long time ago. You have to get past it, Royce. You have to let go of the pain."

"I can't."

"You must."

"I can't, Laura. You don't understand." This was happening all too fast, Royce thought, but even as the warning flashed through his mind, Laura's loving gaze had mesmerized him, seeped into the secrets of his soul and dragged them out over his own traitorous tongue. "When Sabrina died, she was carrying my child."

"You're not falling for him, are you?"

Heaving a sigh, Wendy flounced a hip against the counter of her cluttered mobile home, her voice sharp with the stridence parents use on children who continually misbehave. "Haven't you learned anything from the past three years, Laura? There is no Prince Charming ready to sweep you from a life of drudgery to luxuries beyond compare. There's only 'them,' the rich and powerful who destroy lives with the snap of a money clip, and 'us,' the everyday peons struggling to survive in a world we have no control over.''

Laura twirled her glass of iced tea on the crowded mobile home counter, unwilling to meet her friend's frustrated gaze. ''Royce isn't anything like the Michaelses. He's kind and generous, and gives more money to charity than anyone I've ever met.''

''That's because he has more money than anyone you've ever met. Do you think the Michaelses dropped the custody suit simply out of the goodness of their hearts?'' Wendy flopped a dishrag into the sink with enough force to slop foamy water onto the counter. ''No, they did not. They dropped the lawsuit because a quick comparison of balance sheets showed that they were financially outgunned.''

Even as Laura opened her mouth to dispute that, Royce's comment the night of the gallery opening haunted her. *Power. Control. Money. Whoever has the most, wins.*

A sip of iced tea moistened her throat. ''You don't know what Royce has been through,'' she said finally. ''The pain that he's suffered. He's a good man, Wendy. He cares about people, sincerely cares about them.''

''That's what you said about Donald, until you found out that the only people he cared about were the ones who had something he wanted.'' Wendy paused a beat, then softened her tone. ''Look, hon, I don't want you to get hurt again, that's all. People like you and me, we just can't play ball with the big kids. They might seem nice enough to begin with, but sooner or later they'll steal our lunch money and kick us out of the playground.''

''If it wasn't for Royce, there wouldn't be a playground. He created Burton Tech, turned it into one of the most successful electronics firms in the business, and in doing so put Mill Creek on the industrial map. If not for him, half the people in town would be out of work, including you.''

Wendy paled, turned away and made a production of wiping sloshed dishwater off the counter. ''Speaking of being out of work, there's a rumor going around that the manufacturing facility is going overseas. I don't suppose you know anything about that, do you?''

The question startled Laura, particularly since she'd heard snippets of such a proposal during Royce's discussion with the Marchandt representatives at the gallery opening. Royce hadn't approved the suggestion. Of course, he hadn't disapproved it, either.

Since what she'd heard was confidential, Laura couldn't divulge any of it, not even to her dear friend. ''There's a no-layoff policy at Burton Technologies, isn't there?''

''Policies can be changed.''

''The fact that such a policy exists is proof of how deeply Royce cares about his employees. Do you know that when one of the quality control inspectors suffered a heart attack, Royce not only continued his full salary so he wouldn't have to go on disability, but he also anonymously paid his son's college tuition so the boy wouldn't have to drop out of school?''

Wendy glanced over her shoulder. ''If it was anonymous, how do you know it was Royce who paid it?''

''Marta told me, but that's besides the point.''

''What exactly is the point?'' Wendy asked, shaking detergent bubbles off her hands before snatching up a towel. ''Okay, so you're smitten with the guy. I can understand that. Royce Burton is a hunk and a half. He wasn't touted as one of the state's most eligible bachelors for nothing. I just don't understand why you're suddenly trying to canonize a man we both work for—'' She bit off the words with a gasp, flung the towel aside. ''Oh, my God. You've slept with him.''

Laura felt as if a blowtorch had been applied to her face. Her hands trembled, clinking the ice cubes in her glass. ''You don't happen to have any lemon, do you? Iced tea just isn't the same without a touch of lemon.''

Wendy already circled the counter, plopped onto a stool beside Laura and was digging her fingers into her wrist. ''Tell me I'm wrong. Tell me you haven't completely lost your mind.''

''Do I ask you about your sex life?''

''Of course not, because you know I don't have one. My husband is in Alaska, remember?''

''Say, what time are the boys' soccer games scheduled for tonight? Jamie and I would love to watch them play.''

''Oh, Lord, it's true. You did the deed, and now you think you're in love.'' Moaning, Wendy thunked her forehead on the counter, then spun on the stool and collapsed forward with her elbows on her knees. ''Talk about sleeping with the enemy.''

''Royce Burton is not the enemy.'' Laura set the glass down with a thud, whirled on her hapless friend. ''He's a fine and decent man who rips up thousands of dollars in wine racks to save a stranded kitten, who comforts a crying toddler when he thinks no one is watching, who spends an entire night in the hospital holding a sick woman's hand so she won't be frightened and alone, who secretly sends kids to college, weeps at his mother's grave and still mourns the death of—''

His unborn child.

Horrified to have almost revealed such an intimate secret, Laura simply shut her mouth and turned away.

"He's also your boss," Wendy said, "and a shrewd businessman with a reputation for doing whatever it takes to get what he wants. Certainly he got what he wanted from you."

Straightening her shoulders, Laura faced her friend. "That was a cruel thing to say and unlike you."

"I'm sorry, hon. I wouldn't hurt you for the world."

"You just did."

Wendy sighed, shoved an untidy tousle of hair from her face and poked her tongue into her cheek, a nervous habit that made her look like a chipmunk with mumps. "I'll admit that as tycoons go, Royce Burton is one of the good guys. But you and I both know that no one, and I mean no one, gets to the top in a cutthroat, capitalistic society without cutting a few corners and stomping a few toes. When push comes to shove, he'll do whatever it takes to protect his empire. If that means tossing a few thousand folks into the unemployment line, he'll do it in a heartbeat."

"I don't believe that."

A childish screech from outside diverted Wendy's attention. She went to the screen door and pushed it open. "Tim, quit teasing your brother. Did you hear what I said? Don't make me come out there." Frowning at a muffled response, Wendy started to step onto the porch, then paused to glance over her shoulder. "One of us is wrong about Royce Burton. For your sake, I hope it's me."

"Royce, got a minute?"

"Sure, Dave." Royce slowed his stride down the elegant corporate hallway long enough to allow his financial vice president to catch up. "Where is the revenue forecast report? It should have been on my desk this morning."

"That's what I wanted to talk to you about." Panting slightly, Henderson shifted a stack of folders under his arm and wiped his forehead with the back of his hand. "We're looking at another set of revisions."

"What?" Frowning, Royce returned the greeting of a passing executive with a curt nod, then rounded a corner by the sleek conference room on the way to the executive suite. "Those figures have already been validated by both production and marketing. The reports were scheduled for printing yesterday. We'll need at least two dozen copies for the Marchandt meeting this week."

"I know, but—" Puffing, Henderson rushed his stride to keep up, waiting until they'd entered the private executive suite to complete his sentence. "Have you seen this?"

Royce tossed his copy of the board agenda on his desk and glanced over his shoulder as Dave whipped a magazine from the stack of folders under his arm. "What is it?"

"This week's copy of *Hi-Tech Journal.*"

The glossy trade magazine was considered the bible of the international technologies industry. "I received a copy in the morning mail. I haven't had a chance to read it yet." Taking the proffered copy, he flipped to the index.

"Page twenty-eight," Dave said. "Top paragraph."

Unnerved by the ominous intonation from the usually unflappable executive, Royce skimmed to the page in question with mounting dread.

The moment he saw the first sentence, he knew they

were in trouble. "Has this been verified?" A glance at Henderson's sickly pallor confirmed that it had been. "A Taiwanese firm has been licensed to sell a virtual duplicate of our entire product line and undercut our prices?"

"According to Engineering, they've made just enough minor changes in style to avoid product infringement. According to Legal, we can try for an injunction, but it would only delay the inevitable. According to Marketing, we either lower our prices or prepare to lose a big share of the market."

"How big?"

"We're still forecasting that."

Royce slammed the magazine on his desk. "How big, dammit?"

Henderson's gaze never wavered. "At least forty percent. Probably closer to sixty."

Royce considered that. "Once we get the capital for expansion, economies of scale will allow us to reduce our production costs."

"Not enough. The competition would still be able to undercut our retail prices."

"Perhaps, but after factoring in customer loyalty and trust in the quality of our products, we should be able to maintain most of our current market share."

"Basically."

Keeping his voice steady, Royce forced himself to move slowly around his desk, as if he wasn't the least bit concerned about an occurrence that could spell the beginning of the end of his life's work. "But that isn't going to happen. Marchandt no doubt has the same information we have. Crunch some figures, Dave. Give me the ammunition I need to convince him that no matter what the challenge, our revenues will remain stable.''

Henderson glanced away, shifted his stance. ''Marchandt isn't going to pour millions into any company unless he sees his investment will increase profits, and without the capital to expand, we are all basically screwed. Since we can't project an upswing in revenues, there's only one other way to produce the fiscal result he expects.'' He paused a beat before adding, ''There aren't any options, Royce.''

Seating himself, Royce leaned back in the thick executive chair. ''There are always options.''

''Not this time.''

Swiveling slowly, Royce gazed out the window of his penthouse office to the busy traffic on the street below. In his heart, he knew Dave was right. Royce had run out of options. And he'd run out of time.

Chapter Eleven

Royce descended the stairs with a jaunty bounce, straightening his tie and tugging his cuffs to reveal just the proper amount of fabric below the gray wool sleeve of his suit coat. He swung right at the landing and entered the kitchen. Marta was seated across the table from Jamie, who was kneeling on a chair at the table, spooning cereal into his fat little mouth.

The toddler let out a whoop at Royce's entrance. "Daddy!" he shrieked, spewing droplets of milk across the table. "*My* daddy!"

A swell of sheer happiness exploded inside his chest, as it always did at the sight of the precious child who had claimed a permanent place inside his heart. "Good morning, Jamie. Did you sleep well?"

"Uh-huh."

Scrambling off the chair, Jamie scampered across the room to clutch Royce's knees in a hug, much to

Marta's dismay. "Finish your breakfast, child, before
you ruin Mr. Burton's suit with your sticky fingers."

"It's all right, Marta." Royce scooped Jamie into
his arms and carried him back to the table. There was
a time when his blood pressure would have skyrock-
eted at the sight of a milky stain on his trousers. But
that was before he'd experienced the joy of a child's
affection, the special sweetness of a toddler's hug.
"That's what dry cleaners are for."

The woman frowned as Royce lowered the toddler
into his chair. "It doesn't do much good to teach the
boy manners with you waltzing in, undoing all the lessons."

"You're right, of course." Smiling, he dabbed a
small spot on the knee of his slacks with a napkin, then
rounded the table to plant a kiss atop Marta's curly red
head. It had been nearly three weeks since her surgery,
and she was cranky with boredom. "How are you feeling this morning?"

"Too good to be stuck in my room watching soap
operas." She shifted in her chair as Royce went to fill
his coffee mug. "I'm ready to go back to work."

"As soon as the doctor says you're up to it."

"I'm up to it now."

"Another couple of weeks."

"The house will be condemned for filth by then."

Royce chuckled, then took a sip of hot coffee.
Marta's idea of filth was a minuscule stain in the tile
grout and a speck of dust on the baseboards. "A cleaning crew is scheduled to give the house a spit-and-
polish shine for tonight's dinner party. They have orders to report directly to you."

She brightened. "Do they, now?"

"You're not to tire yourself. Simply give them instructions and make certain they've performed each task to your satisfaction.''

''What about Laura?''

He angled a wary glance. ''What about her?''

Marta regarded him with an expression that he couldn't quite decipher. ''She's in charge of tonight's little soiree. I wouldn't want to step on her toes.''

Royce smiled, knowing perfectly well how miffed Marta was that Laura had taken over so many of her duties while she recuperated. ''It was Laura's idea. Besides, I happen to know that you've been the brains behind the scene for all the preparations. Laura told me that she wouldn't have known where to start if you hadn't given her such detailed instructions.''

''She said that?'' Clearly surprised, Marta raised her brows, then lowered them suspiciously. ''Pillow talk, I suppose.''

A swallow of coffee backed up in his throat. He coughed, then set the cup aside. ''Excuse me?''

The woman sighed and glanced away. ''Footsteps vibrate the ceiling of my quarters every night, and first thing every morning. You smiling all the time, and her glowing like sunshine's stuck to her skin. I may be old, but I'm not a fool.''

Royce glanced at Jamie, who was happily smearing milky finger pictures across the table. ''Even if my private life was your business, which it isn't, this is not the place to discuss it.''

Sadness clouded her eyes. ''She'll hurt you.''

''That's enough,'' he snapped, with enough edge to startle the toddler. Royce straightened and lowered his voice. ''You will not broach this topic again. Not with me, not with Laura, not with anyone. Is that understood?''

Averting her gaze, Marta bit her lower lip and nodded.

Royce pivoted on his heel, strode out of the kitchen and crossed the foyer. As he rounded the corner adjacent to his study, he nearly collided with Laura.

She gasped at his appearance and held a black object she'd been fiddling with behind her back. "What are you doing here?"

"I live here."

She flushed prettily. "I thought you had an early meeting at the office."

"And so I do. As soon as I retrieve my briefcase, I'll be off." He leaned to the side, trying to peer behind her back. "What have you got there?"

"You mean this?" Holding out a camera, she gazed up with wide, innocent eyes. "I was, ah, just going to get some photos of Jamie having his breakfast."

Smiling, Royce caressed her cheek with his thumb. God, she was beautiful, so radiant and luminescent. Marta was right. She did look like a woman with sunshine stuck to her skin. "You may want to hold off on that. He's a bit untidy at the moment."

Her laugh was a bit too bright. "That's the joy of parenthood. Capturing those special moments of one's child wearing his breakfast in his hair." She gazed up with eyes the color of new spring grass, and lips moist as a dewy morning. "You've got milk on your cheek," she murmured, slipping her arms around his waist.

"A kiss from Jamie." He gathered her in his embrace, noticing her cast a wary glance back toward the foyer. "Marta is in the kitchen."

She flushed, smiled, absorbed the small droplet on his cheek with her fingertip. "It seems so peculiar that we must display affection in public and conceal it at home. I wish—'' Frowning, she bit her lip and fell silent.

''What do you wish? Tell me and it's yours.''

Laura allowed him to tilt her face upward and was rewarded by the warmth in eyes glowing like polished amber. She wished that the fantasy was real, that she could whisper that she loved him beyond measure, that she desired him beyond reason, that all she ever dreamed of, all she ever dared hope for was right here in the cradle of his arms.

In her heart, she believed that he cared deeply for her, although he'd never said so. In her mind, however, pragmatism took over. Royce Burton was a magnificent lover, but he was also a man who recognized opportunity and turned it to his advantage. She had gone willingly to his bed because she loved him, yet she held no illusions that he returned that coveted emotion. Perhaps what they'd shared meant as much to him as it did to her; perhaps he merely considered their lovemaking a pleasant diversion.

The power of her own emotion awed her, frightened her. She saw in Royce a man of strength, of principle, of secret sadness and concealed compassion. But she'd also seen her first husband as kind and vulnerable, when in reality he'd been merely weak and needy. Laura was afraid to trust herself, afraid to trust her own judgment, particularly when her heart was involved.

''Laura?'' A worried veil dampened the warm glow in his eyes. ''Is something wrong?''

''No.'' Her smile was genuine, pushing doubt into a distant corner of her mind. One thing she had learned in her life was to live for the moment, and cherish each joy as if it were the last happiness of her life. Because it very well could be. "Everything is fine. In fact, everything is absolutely wonderful."

A glimmer of relief peeked through the wary veil of his gaze and softened the tension of his jaw. "Then what is it you wish for? Tell me, and I'll have it brought to you on a satin pillow."

She laughed at his teasing tone. "Ooh, that would be a sight! Actually, I was wishing that you didn't have to go to work so I could drag you back to bed and make mad, passionate love to you." Moistening her lips with exaggerated sensuality, she danced her fingertips along his belt. "After a few minutes of my tender ministrations, I rather doubt that what I wish for would even fit on that pillow."

He actually blushed. "You flatter me."

"Get the pillow, and let's check it out."

A hearty laugh warmed her to the bone. "You amaze me, Laura, you really do. Every time I think I have you all figured out, you do or say something so incredibly unexpected that I am taken completely by surprise."

"Women do not like to be figured out." She smoothed the lapels of his suit jacket and straightened his tie. The intimacy of the proprietary gestures sent a cadre of goose bumps marching down her arms. "We like to keep men guessing. It's our nature to be mysterious and provocative."

"You are that," he murmured, bending his head to nuzzle her ear. "And so much more."

She shivered at the exquisite sensation, tilting her head to allow his lips access to the sensitive pulse of her throat. Of their own volition, her hands slipped under his jacket to press against the corded strength of his back. A soft sigh slipped from her lips, and she nearly dropped the camera.

When Royce finally pulled himself away his pupils had dilated to obsidian darkness, and he was breathing hard. "If I don't leave now, I never will."

"I could live with that," she murmured. "But I suppose I should behave myself since you have a business to run." Heaving a breath, she turned to watch him enter the study. "What time will you be home?"

"What time will the dinner party start?"

"Dinner is at 8:00 p.m., but the first guests will probably be arriving by seven."

He snagged his briefcase from the desk and slipped his cell phone into his pocket. "I'll be home by six."

"Will that give you enough time to shower and change?"

"It will unless you plan to join me." He flashed an evil grin, passed through the study doorway and wrapped an arm around her waist. "If you do plan to join me, I'll be home by five."

"Make it four," she whispered, raising her lips for his kiss. "Better yet, make it three. I have plans for you."

"I can't wait."

After a sweet kiss that lingered as long as it dared, Royce hoisted his briefcase and strode out the front door. Laura ran to the foyer window. As soon as his vehicle pulled out of the massive circular driveway, she extracted the film from her camera and tucked it safely in her purse.

She had big plans for that, too.

By one o'clock, the house was in chaos, with work crews setting up expansion tables in the dining room and smaller hors d'oeuvre buffets in the parlor.

Laura quickly signed one delivery invoice, while Marta stepped in front of a deliveryman carrying a wine crate. "Open it," she demanded. The fellow set the crate down, pulled a small pry bar from his pocket and did as requested. Marta pulled a bottle from the straw nest and squinted at the label. "Where's the chardonnay?"

"We've got ten more crates in the truck." He nodded toward the open front door. "Merlot, sauvignon, zinfandel, chardonnay and some vintage port."

Laura glanced up. "The wet bar in the entertainment room has already been fully stocked. There are some temporary wine tables set up in the parlor, but even so we won't have enough space for that many bottles."

"We'll store it in the cellar," Marta replied. "The servers can bring up the bottles as needed."

"That's a good idea." Handing the clipboard back to the furniture deliveryman, Laura went to open the basement door for the fellow struggling with the wine crate. He smiled his appreciation as she flipped a switch to illuminate the basement stairs. "Watch your step."

"Yes'm." The fellow took a deep breath and disappeared into the bowels of the cellar.

Laura returned to the foyer in time to see Marta directing the florist, who had just entered carrying one of the many autumn-themed centerpieces for the buffet tables. "When will the caterers be here?"

"Hmm?" Marta glanced over her shoulder, eyes shining. Clearly the woman was in her element and enjoying every moment of the party preparations. "The caterers will be here by five. The chamber music quartet will arrive around the same time. We'll set them up in the parlor... Hey!'' Marta wiggled a finger at the florist, who was circling the area with a befuddled expression. ''That arrangement is for the main buffet in the dining room. That way.''

Marta jerked a thumb in the proper direction. The confused fellow wandered off just as an ominous hiss emanated from the basement, followed by a bellow of terror.

''Oh, my God,'' Laura mumbled. ''Maggie.''

She spun on her heel, dashed through the basement door and descended the winding stairs to find the deliveryman with his back to the wall, clutching his wine crate and surrounded by frolicking kittens that leaped on his shoes and dug their tiny claws into his leg as they climbed it like a handy tree.

Blocking his exit was a growling mama cat, whose fur stood out as if each hair had been individually starched. Clearly, Maggie did not appreciate the intrusion into her feline nursery.

''Help me!'' the horrified man shouted as one of the bright-eyed kittens climbed upward, nearing a sensitive portion of his anatomy. ''Get these blood-thirsty monsters off!''

Laura dashed forward, plucking Rascal off the fellow's thigh and Cary Grant off his knee. ''I'm so sorry.'' She tucked both kittens in the empty barrel that was frequently used for kitten containment, then set about gathering the rest of the brood. ''I forgot all about the kittens. It didn't occur to me that they'd be a bother.''

He set down the crate and yanked up his pants leg to examine a row of tiny scratches. ''They're a damned menace.''

Maggie hissed.

"Stop that," Laura scolded. "You should be ashamed of yourself." She scooped Maggie up and placed her in with the kittens, knowing that the mama cat would remove her brood from the barrel as soon as she considered it safe to do so.

She cleared her throat. "I do apologize. The kittens were just being playful, but apparently Maggie was, er, upset by your howling."

The fellow stared up in disbelief. "You'd howl, too, if your legs were being shredded."

"Yes, I imagine I would. Is there anything I can do for you?"

He shoved his pants leg down with a snort. "Just keep those needle-clawed shrews away from me while I finish my delivery."

"They'll stay in the barrel until you're through," Laura assured him, hoping it was true. "Just stack the crates over in that corner, please."

The fellow shot her a look, then transported the crate as instructed before trudging back up the stairs, mumbling to himself.

Laura shifted a glance toward the barrel and saw a pair of twitchy orange ears and two yellow eyes peering out. "If you value your naps on Royce's burgundy lounge chair, you'll stay put, do you hear? And teach your babies some manners while you're at it. Using human legs for a scratching post is dreadfully impolite." Maggie issued a mew that Laura chose to interpret as contrite, despite the fact that her cat eyes sparked with a distinct lack of remorse. "I'm glad we understand each other."

Maggie blinked but offered no argument, so Laura reluctantly mounted the stairs just as Marta appeared in the doorway. "Some place called One Hour Photo called. Your prints are—" she spun around as Laura headed toward the front door "—ready."

It was the last word Laura heard as she dashed past the wine man carrying another crate up the walkway and ran toward her car. The prints were ready. She was so excited she could barely fit the key in the ignition.

Her plan was finally coming to fruition.

"A beautiful boy, Burton."

Jamie giggled and wrapped his pudgy, warm arms around Royce's neck. "My daddy," he announced, then stuffed his fingers in his mouth and drooled with delight.

Issuing a jovial chuckle, André Marchandt swirled a snifter of amber cognac, beaming his approval. His gaze slipped from the toddler in Royce's arms to the gorgeous blonde at his side. "And a magnificent wife," he added, speaking with a lilting hint of Continental accent. "You must be very proud."

"Indeed I am," Royce murmured, dabbing Jamie's moist chin with a handkerchief.

"It is what a successful man needs," Marchandt continued. "An heir for the family fortune and a lovely woman to keep the home fires burning, eh?"

From the corner of his eye, Royce saw Laura flinch at Marchandt's blatant inspection. Not that Royce blamed him. Laura was breathtaking, exquisitely gowned in an ankle-length sheath of black satin that dipped low enough to reveal a hint of cleavage in the front, and bared her lovely back to the waist. A chic web of corded silk crisscrossed her magnificent shoulder blades. Her hair was a tantalizing twist of curls piled atop her head, studded with glimmering pearls and accented by wispy tendrils that teased her high cheekbones, framing her delicate features with elegance and style.

Royce wanted to yank out the pearl pins, run his fingers through the tangled locks and have her right there on the parlor floor. He imagined that every other man in the room possessed the same fantasy.

As Marchandt's cool blue gaze fastened on Laura's chest, she held out her hand with a hospitable smile. "Welcome to our home, Mr. Marchandt. Royce has spoken of you so often, I feel as if we're old friends." Despite her obvious discomfort, she held her chin up with regal grace, managing not to cringe when the stocky European snagged her proffered hand to kiss the inside of her wrist with a bit too much enthusiasm.

"The pleasure," he mumbled against her skin, "is for me."

Jamie shifted in Royce's arms, observing the wrist-kissing ritual with somber interest. When Marchandt finally relinquished his prize, he turned to beam at the staring toddler. "Ah, you look just like your papa."

Royce shifted uncomfortably, recalling that the child's resemblance was the main reason he'd suggested the marital charade in the first place. If Jamie had been blond and blue-eyed, Royce realized how very different his life would have been, and how much joy he would have missed.

"Yes, indeed." Marchandt took another sip of cognac and smacked his lips. "You are quite the handsome child."

Jamie eyed him for a moment. "You fat."

The announcement stiffened Royce's spine and widened Marchandt's eyes. Beside him, Laura instantly stepped forward to take the pajama-clad toddler out of Royce's arms. "It's bedtime, Jamie—"

"Fat man!" the baby chortled, clapping like a happy seal.

"No, no, sweetie, that's not nice." Clearly horrified, Laura shifted the toddler to her shoulder and turned apologetically to the stunned investment broker. "I'm so sorry, Mr. Marchandt."

Royce held his breath as the man's icy eyes blinked twice. Then to his shock, Marchandt burst into laughter. "Ah, but the child is correct. I am fat." He elbowed one of his gray-suited lackeys, pointed to Jamie and chuckled so hard his round belly vibrated. "Do you hear what he say? A brave youngster, no? He speaks his mind."

The man paled, swallowed hard. "Yes, sir."

"I like that boy," Marchandt said, still grinning. "He's got, how you say, gumption."

"Yes, sir."

Offering a weak smile, Royce glanced around the room until he saw Marta hovering by one of the buffet tables scolding a chagrined server who was balancing a tray of hors d'oeuvres.

Royce caught the housekeeper's eye, motioned her over at the same time a movement at the skirt of the table caught his attention. As he watched, the movement slipped along the length of the cloth-draped table, where the pleated fabric brushed the carpet.

Apparently Laura saw the table skirt vibrate the same moment. She frowned, nudged Royce with her shoulder and nodded toward the peculiar occurrence.

He shrugged, was distracted as Marta joined them. "Jamie is ready for bed," he told the woman, who smiled with delight when the baby held out his chubby arms to her.

Since Marta hadn't fully recuperated from her surgery, Laura stood the child on the floor instead.

"No, no, sweetie, Marta can't carry you. You hold her hand, okay?"

"Okay." Jamie took Marta's hand and toddled off. He paused at the parlor doorway, looked back toward the buffet table and giggled. "Bye, kitty."

Royce and Laura looked at each other, then followed the child's gaze in time to see a cocktail weenie disappear under the edge of the table skirt. A moment later, a meatball squirted out, followed by a scampering black-and-white kitten. The kitten batted the meatball across the floor, past a pair of high-heeled lamé pumps, over the polished toe of a formal dress brogue.

A high-pitched gasp revealed that the tiny animal's antics had not gone unnoticed by some of the guests. The woman in the gold lamé pumps stepped aside, staring down with stunned dismay. The owner of the polished dress brogues bent to dab gravy off his shoe with a cocktail napkin, eyeing the antics of the pirouetting kitten with obvious befuddlement.

When a tiny ball of orange fur peeked out from behind a salad bowl atop the buffet table, Laura's eyes popped so wide Royce feared they might fall out.

"Ah…" She shot a panicked glance at Royce, then turned a strained smile on Marchandt. "Will you excuse me for a moment?"

"Of course, my dear."

As Marchandt turned to watch the sway of her hips, Royce flung an arm around the fat fellow's shoulders and spun him around. "So, how about those Mets?"

Marchandt blinked.

* * *

Frantic, Laura managed to scoop the orange kitten from behind the salad bowl, but not soon enough to prevent the clam-dipped paw prints encircling the steaming platters of appetizers and finger foods. "Oh, Sam," she murmured. "Look what you've done."

A glance at Royce confirmed that he'd aimed Marchandt away from the chaos, and was trying to shuffle him out the parlor door. By the time she looked back, Dave Henderson had snagged a morsel from the rumaki platter.

Laura gasped, grabbed his wrist just before he popped it into his mouth. She shook her head, then nodded toward the paw prints on the tablecloth and rolled her gaze down to the squirming kitten she was unsuccessfully attempting to conceal in her folded arms. He paled visibly, replaced the rumaki and snapped his fingers to garner the attention of a nearby waiter.

"Please stay here until I return," Laura whispered. "And for heaven's sake, don't let anyone eat anything."

As Laura turned, she was face-to-face with a silver-haired woman wearing a cascade of dripping diamonds on her earlobes and a perplexed smile. "I believe this is yours?"

Laura groaned as the woman held out a fluffy white kitten with barbecue sauce on its whiskers and paws.

Mortified beyond description, Laura gathered the mewing Bunny-Cat in her arms. "I'm so sorry, Mrs. Wyncroft. I have no idea how this could have happened."

Mrs. Wyncroft's eyes twinkled. "My dear Sassy-Cat

had kittens last year. They are such creative little creatures, aren't they?''

"Yes," she murmured, trying to hold two squirming animals. "They are."

"Is there something I can do to help?"

"Ah, well—"

A high-pitched shriek spun Laura around just as a well-dressed woman in a glimmering cocktail dress leapt up from Royce's antique, Philadelphia-style settee as if she'd been burned. When she spun around, screaming wildly, Laura saw Rascal clinging to her rhinestone-studded derriere like a furry tick.

The woman's male companion hesitated a moment before attempting to extract the stubborn creature, a rather delicate procedure considering the personal location to which the kitten had affixed itself.

Conversation around the room ceased. Even the chamber music stopped, as the quartet lowered their instruments and joined the guests in watching with rapt fascination as Rascal the cat leapt from the shrieking woman's bottom to scurry under a nearby chair.

Clearly, discretion was no longer an option. "There are two more around here somewhere," Laura confessed. "Maybe three. At this point, any assistance at all would be most appreciated."

The woman's society smile broadened into a conspiratorial grin. "Garth and I have just returned from a safari," she said, gesturing toward a sleek, balding gentleman in a svelte dinner jacket. "If we can track lions across the savannah, we can certainly capture a couple of kittens in a parlor."

Garth stepped forward, trying desperately not to smile at the tiny black face peering out from under the buffet table skirt. "I believe I see my quarry now."

With that, he dropped to his knees as if he were clad in dungarees instead of sharply creased trousers, and shimmied under the table with the enthusiastic delight of an eight-year-old chasing pond frogs.

"The hunt is on," Mrs. Wyncroft said with a conspiratorial wink. "My, I haven't had this much fun since the mailman tripped the automatic sprinklers."

A guttural groan caught in Laura's throat. She managed a thin smile, clutched the two wriggling kittens and rushed toward the doorway, pausing by Marchandt, who was watching the pandemonium with goggle-eyed glee.

She turned to Royce, who simply bit his lower lip and stared down at her.

"I'm so sorry," she whispered.

His lip quivered, his eyes sparkled, his chest vibrated strangely.

"I've ruined everything…" She squinted up at him. "Are you laughing?"

He shook his head with too much force to be believed.

"Yes, you are." The gurgle of a giggle rolled around her own chest until she glanced over her shoulder and saw a woman in a diamond tiara wandering aimlessly around the room with a black kitten cupped between her bejeweled fingers.

The giggle turned into a groan as Laura realized that the entire dinner party had disintegrated into utter disaster. She hurried into the foyer and saw what she'd feared. The basement door was wide open, apparently left in that position for the convenience of the bartenders who were ferrying wine bottles from the cellar.

A white-jacketed server emerged carrying two wine bottles. Laura spun him around as she rushed past, descending the stairs and popping the two kittens into the empty barrel. A glance around the basement revealed that the window was ajar, as usual, and Maggie was nowhere in sight.

So much for kitten-collecting the easy way. Without Maggie to retrieve her brood, the human population was on its own.

Without pausing to catch her breath, Laura hurried back upstairs and was greeted by André Marchandt himself, who stood in the doorway holding Cary Grant in his arms. Behind him, a laughing line of guests wound into the parlor, passing little Rascal from one set of hands to another in the feline version of shuttling sandbags from one disaster area to another.

Marchandt affectionately stroked Cary Grant's sleek black fur. "I must confess, Mrs. Burton, that I have never cared much for dinner parties," he said. "This is one occasion, however, that I shall never forget."

"I'm sure," Laura murmured, accepting the proffered kitten. With a thin smile, she hurried down the basement stairs to tuck Cary Grant into the kitten barrel.

When she returned to the basement doorway, Rascal was neatly nested in Marchandt's arms, and Bunny-Cat was in the process of being handed from one guest to another. Laura scooped up both kittens and headed down to the basement.

After tucking Rascal and Bunny-Cat into the kitten barrel, she returned for Sam and Patches, the tiny calico with sticky white paws that smelled suspiciously of clam dip.

When the final kitten had been safely tucked away, she closed the basement door with a forceful snap and was immediately treated to a round of applause from the guests, all of whom had gathered in the foyer, flushed with laugher and the exertion of their kitten safari.

Since there was little else to do, Laura took a bow.

"Ladies and gentlemen," she said with more bravado than she felt. "You'll be pleased to know that dinner is now being served in our feline-free dining room."

There was another round of applause, punctuated with a roar of appreciative laughter.

As the crowd moved toward the dining area, Royce appeared at her side. "Mrs. Burton, you certainly know how to throw a party."

She tucked her hand beneath his elbow. "If you think that was wild, wait until you see what I've planned for later this evening."

"Would this perchance be a private event?"

"Very private."

He brushed her cheek with a kiss. "I have to spend a few minutes with Marchandt after the other guests leave. After that, the night belongs to us."

If happiness was fatal, Laura would have expired on the spot. All her life she'd wondered if romantic love truly existed, or if it was merely the figment of a fiction writer's imagination.

Finally she had her answer.

Impatiently pacing the master suite, Laura glanced at the clock radio. It was nearly 1:00 a.m. The last guest had left two hours ago, and Royce had been holed up in his study with Marchandt ever since.

For the third time in fifteen minutes, she paused in front of the mirror to check her makeup and straighten the frothy negligee she'd purchased for a special evening. Tonight would be incredibly special. She felt it in her bones.

A shiver slipped down her spine, chilling her.

Instinct propelled her into the hallway. She listened, heard no sound from the lower floor and wondered if the business meeting was over. It wouldn't be the first time Royce had closed his eyes for a moment and fallen asleep in the study.

She tiptoed down the stairs, hiding in the shadows lest her intimate apparel be spotted by anyone except the loving man for whom it was intended.

Light shone from beneath the closed study door.

Laura sidled to a nearby doorway and stealthily eased toward the study, listening for voices that would alert to her that the meeting was still in session.

To her dismay, she heard voices. And when she realized what those voices were saying, her entire world collapsed.

Chapter Twelve

"Daddy! My daddy!" Squealing with delight at Royce's appearance in the kitchen, Jamie squirmed while his mother gamely tried to wipe oatmeal off his face.

"Good morning, little man."

Royce couldn't keep from smiling, nor could he prevent himself from responding when the toddler stood up on the chair with outstretched arms. He scooped the child up, kissed his damp cheek, then turned to Laura, who averted her gaze. There was a harsh edge to the line of her mouth that bothered him.

He regarded her warily. "You were asleep when I came upstairs last night."

"It was late. I was tired." She stepped away, crossed the kitchen and made a production of rinsing the face-cloth in the sink.

An odd sense of uneasiness moved through him. "Is that why you slept in the guest room?"

"I slept in my quarters, if that's what you mean. Under the terms of our contract, I'm entitled to that private space." She folded the facecloth on the counter and busied herself rinsing cereal bowls. "I have an early appointment this morning. I hope you won't mind making other arrangements for your breakfast."

Frowning, he carried the squirming toddler across the room. "It's Saturday. I don't recall seeing anything on your schedule for this morning."

"I'm not required to inform you about how I spend my personal time."

When she turned around to take Jamie out of his arms, the desolation in her eyes turned his sense of disquiet into an icy lump of fear. "You're not upset about last night's dinner party, are you? I know it didn't turn out exactly as you'd planned, but—"

"The cleaning crew will be here by 9:00 a.m. to shovel the place out." Laura shifted Jamie in her arms just as Marta appeared in the doorway, yawning and tying her bathrobe sash. "Marta will supervise them."

Marta blinked at the sound of her name. She opened her mouth, then prudently clamped it shut again, clearly affected by the tension in the room. Glancing from Royce to Laura and back again, she poured herself a cup of coffee and sat at the table without saying a word.

Perplexed and worried by Laura's sudden distance, Royce slipped a sideways glance at Marta, then opted to pretend that nothing was amiss. "I cleared my own schedule this morning, hoping that you and Jamie might enjoy a boat trip out on the lake. There's a cabin cruiser I was thinking of purchasing—"

"I don't like boats. I can't swim, and I get seasick." Laura turned to Marta. "Jamie and I will be out most of the day. Don't hold dinner for us."

As she turned toward the door, Royce stopped her. "I don't understand, Laura. Where are you going?"

She studied him with an expression of supreme sadness. "To look for an apartment."

"What?" He yanked his hand from her arm as if the touch of her skin had burned him. "But why?"

"The terms of our contract have been fulfilled. Jamie and I are leaving."

That's when he saw the contempt in her eyes, and realized that she knew about the deal he'd cut with Marchandt.

Laura stood beside the study window, gazing out at the manicured lawn. Outside, Jamie scampered in the morning sunshine, while Marta lounged beneath the patio umbrella, watching him play. Her heart felt as if it had been scraped raw.

Life's lessons were either learned or repeated. Laura, it seemed, was not the most apt student. She should have known better than to trust a man like Royce Burton.

She should have known better than to love him.

On the surface, Royce was polished and poised, a man who could be both tender and generous when it suited his purpose. Deep down, however, he was no different from any of the other rich and powerful people who had wreaked havoc on her life, people whose self-esteem centered around power over others.

Now Royce stood behind her, hovering in the center of the very study where he'd planned the annihilation of an entire town.

He cleared his throat. "It's just business, Laura. Sometimes difficult decisions have to be made for the greater good."

She fingered the venetian blinds, tilting her head to watch Jamie chase a fat beach ball across the lawn. "Funny how that 'greater good' always results in the rich getting richer at the expense of everyone else."

"There isn't any choice, Laura. Without the capital to expand, Burton Tech can't remain competitive. The company will fold, and all those jobs you're so concerned about will be lost forever."

"So you're simply going to jump-start that loss by closing down the manufacturing operation and relocating the corporate offices to Manhattan." It was a statement, not a question, since Laura had overheard details of the plan quite clearly last night. She extracted her fingertip from the blinds and folded her arms tightly. "Thousands of people will be out of work here in Mill Creek, Royce, people who will have to pack up and leave to find jobs."

"We'll subsidize the moving expenses of any employees who want to follow the company to New York City."

She turned, studying the tight lines creasing his forehead and the ridges of his mouth. "That takes care of about ten percent of the company's employees, those who work in the corporate offices. What about the others? Are you going to send them to those new overseas manufacturing plants to work for a tenth of their current wages?"

A muscle in his jaw clenched. "You have to consider the overview and long-term results. The expansion will allow for thousands upon thousands of more jobs overall."

"Jobs in Asia, or South America, or Europe, or even in New York City, but not here in Mill Creek." Laura shifted away from the window, gazing at the stacks of papers cluttering his desk. "How will that help Wendy and her sons, Royce? They're barely making ends meet now. What will happen to them when she loses her job?"

"She'll find another one."

"Where, Royce? At the diner down the street? Not likely. The diner depends on shift workers from the plant. As soon as the manufacturing plant closes, so will the diner. And as people leave town searching for work, the hardware store will close, and the bank, and the boutique over on Main Street, and all the small businesses that have turned Mill Creek into a vibrant, healthy community."

A flash of sorrow passed through his gaze before he blinked it away. He turned his back, instantly angering her.

She rounded the desk, grabbed his arm and spun him around. "And what about all those homes that will suddenly be up for sale, Royce? Who will be left to buy them? Real estate values will plummet. People will declare bankruptcy. The town will die, Royce. There will be nothing left except boarded-up houses and broken dreams."

"It's necessary."

"Yes, it's necessary. Necessary in order for you to maintain your own wealth and power."

He blanched, flexed his fingers. "Is that what you think of me?"

"What else can I think?" She felt as if she'd swallowed a brick. "I heard Marchandt offer you a deal. He'll give you the money to turn Burton Technologies into a global power, with you at the helm. He dangled the carrot. You grabbed it. All you have to do now is betray your employees, sell out your friends, destroy your town and hand your soul to the devil.''

With every word, Royce's complexion paled another notch until his dark eyes flashed from a face as white as a snowbank. ''You can believe what you want to believe, Laura. I can't stop you. But while you're busy pillorying me in your mind, try to conceive, if it's possible, the end result of refusing Marchandt's offer.''

Unnerved by the intensity of his gaze, Laura stepped back but was stopped when Royce took hold of her wrist.

''Do you think all this—'' his gaze encompassed the room, the house, the entire town with a sweep of his hand ''—just miraculously happened? Only one in ten thousand new businesses even survive the first year, let alone thrives and grows for more than a decade. Beating those odds took years and years of work, of planning, of taking risks and staying one step ahead of everyone else. It took an understanding of technology and global economics, and the courage to make the correct adjustments years before anyone else realized that an adjustment was even needed. If it wasn't for me, Mill Creek would still be a poverty zone, with more tractors than cars and kids who hiked to school with holes in their shoes.''

She yanked her wrist from his grasp. ''So now you get to play God? The Lord giveth and the Lord taketh away?''

He vibrated as if struck and rocked back a step. ''If we don't make this expansion move now, everything you've predicted for Mill Creek will still come to pass, because Burton Technologies will be out of business inside of three years.''

"Based on what, a guesswork marketing forecast?"

"Yes, damn it, based on forecasts and projections that indicate quite clearly that by the end of this year, rip-offs of our products will be available on the consumer market at a price that undercuts us by at least twenty percent. Our manufacturing process is labor intensive, which means that we have to cut labor costs just to stay competitive. Do you think my employees are so loyal that they'd willingly work for less than industry standard?" He snatched a bound report off his desk, shook it as if it were a snake, then flung it back with enough force that it skimmed the polished surface and plopped onto the floor. "Hell, no, they won't. If I tried to cut their wages, they'd form a union and shut down the entire operation in five minutes flat."

"How do you know? Have you asked them?"

Her soft question came as he was raking his hair in frustration. His fingers paused, tangled in his hair much as her own had been so often over the past weeks. Flashes of their lovemaking jittered through her tormented mind, memories of the wildness, the passion, the tenderness of their joining.

There had been magic in their union, a mating of heart and soul that Laura had never experienced before. And would never experience again.

It was over. She knew it. He knew it.

Laura hated what Royce was planning, but she still understood it. Everything he was, everything he believed himself to be was inextricably entwined with the success of the company that he'd created from his own blood, sweat and tears.

Burton Technologies was a livelihood to thousands,

but it was Royce's entire life. It was the reality of acceptance to the poor child that still lived inside him, the child of a desperate mother and a father who hadn't cared enough to remain a part of his son's world. To Royce, success was the measure of worth as a man. To fail, to lose the company that mirrored his own sense of self-worth would be more devastating to him than the loss of a limb, or the loss of his own life.

Wendy had been right about Royce. To him power was everything; he'd do whatever it took to maintain his grasp on it, and to keep that frightened, hungry little boy of his childhood at bay.

Once again, Laura had fallen in love with a man she'd misjudged, a man who had the power to control her life, and the power to destroy it.

"The contract provisions only oblige Jamie and I to stay in your home until the partnership agreement has been certified," she said. "We'll be leaving by the end of the week."

A flux of emotion flashed through Royce's eyes. "Where will you go?"

"Does it matter?"

The emotion drained from his gaze, leaving only the blank stare she'd seen the first time she'd met him. He squared his shoulders, then clasped his hands behind his back. "No, I suppose it doesn't."

"I told you she was up to no good." Huffing, Marta placed a stack of messages on Royce's desk, tapping the top message with her fingertip. "She got what she wanted, and then some."

Wearily, Royce swiveled in his chair and regarded the woman who had traveled the roughest roads life had to offer right alongside him. It had been nearly a week since the dinner party where Laura had learned the catastrophic result of his expansion plans. The deal still hadn't been signed, however. Royce kept sending the papers back to the legal department for insignificant changes. He didn't know why.

"Laura kept her end of the bargain," he told Marta. "I'll keep mine."

Marta issued a snort. "Was wrapping your heart around her finger and soaking you for every luxury she could get her hands on part of the bargain?"

"My heart is perfectly fine," he lied. "It's also none of your business."

"You're my business. I promised your mama I'd watch out for you and that's exactly what I plan to do." She snatched up one of the messages, held it out until he took it from her.

"What's this?"

"It's a message from the most expensive jewelry shop in town. It seems that Mrs. Burton's—" she pronounced Laura's married name with enhanced sarcasm "—special order is ready."

"So?"

"So she just had to get herself one last hunk of your wallet," Marta said. "Ordered herself a fine piece of jewelry, kind of like a going-away present to herself, I'd wager. After all, she'll be needing some fancy trimmings to go with those expensive designer duds you bought for her."

"She bought those clothes for herself." Royce wadded the message, flung it into the trash. "A deduction has been taken from her paycheck each week to cover the cost of garments necessary for her…position."

The information clearly startled Marta. She blinked, then frowned.

Royce scoured his eyelids with his fingertips. "Call the jewelry store. Have Laura's order delivered and see that she receives it immediately."

Issuing a curt nod, the woman turned to leave. She paused at the doorway. "You didn't let yourself fall for her, did you?"

Royce leveled a cool stare in her direction. "Please close the door on your way out."

"The rumors are all over the plant," Wendy said, laying her napkin beside her luncheon plate. "Everyone is scared to death."

Laura reached for the check, dug into her handbag. "You know I can't discuss it, Wendy. Please, don't ask me."

"But you have to know something." Wendy gripped Laura's wrist as she laid the cash on the small money tray. "I'm your best friend. You owe me the truth."

Tears heated Laura's eyes. She bit her lower lip and clutched Wendy's hand across the linen-clad table. "I owe you everything. If not for you, Jamie and I might have starved in the street. What you're asking is not just that I betray a confidence. You want me to violate the terms of an agreement that will give my son the security he deserves to live a safe and happy life. Please, you have to understand."

Wendy stiffened. "I'm a mother, Laura. Of course I understand. I'd run you or anyone else through with a saber before I'd allow my own children to be hurt. But…" She gnawed her lip and touched her chin with fingers that trembled. "I'm just so scared, that's all. If I lose my job, Daniel will have to stay in Alaska for at least another year. We won't be able to afford the mobile home, and there's no room for the kids and me in that communal ward of oil riggers where Daniel is living. I don't know what we'll do, Laura. I just don't know what we'll do.''

"I know.'' Exhaling all at once, Laura slumped in the thickly padded chair and glanced around the bustling restaurant that was the finest in all of Mill Creek. If Royce had his way, this would all be gone soon, nothing but a fond memory of glory days from a crumbling ghost town.

Wendy went white. "It's true, isn't it? The plant is going to be closed down.''

Without a word, Laura revealed the truth in her eyes.

Wendy swallowed a small sob and twisted the napkin in her hand. "So, if you were me, would you start sending out résumés?''

"Yes.''

Nodding, Wendy slumped back against her chair, wiping her forehead with the back of her hand. She gazed into space for a moment. "Maybe this isn't such a bad thing after all.''

"What do you mean?''

"Maybe this will force Daniel and I to slow down long enough to realize what our quest for financial security has done to our family.'' Wendy sighed, regarding Laura with a sad smile. "I miss my husband, hon. I'd rather live in an igloo with a whole family than live in a mansion with half of one.''

A lump wedged in Laura's throat. "I can understand that.''

"I just never wanted my sons to feel as if they couldn't have the same things their friends had, you know? And I want my sons to go to college, get a good education. All that costs money.'' After a moment, Wendy emitted a thin laugh. "You know, a few years ago there were rumors that the employees were going to be offered a profit-sharing incentive. Too bad that one was false.''

''Why?''

Wendy shrugged. ''Because if the employees had had the opportunity to buy shares of the company back then, we'd probably have enough stock by now to vote down the merger and keep our jobs... Laura? What's wrong? You look positively catatonic.''

''Hmm? Oh, nothing.'' She snatched up her purse and slid out of the chair. ''Finish your coffee, hon. I've got to go.''

''Go?'' Clearly bewildered, Wendy pushed away from the table. ''Go where?''

''To start another rumor.''

Chapter Thirteen

"May I come in?"

Royce spun around in his chair and automatically stood as Laura hovered in the doorway. "Yes, of course."

His heart pounded as she entered the study tentatively, pausing only to smile at the lazy orange cat lounging in the burgundy recliner. Her smile froze into a grimace, as if a sad thought had struck her.

After a moment's hesitation, she seated herself on the settee at the far side of the spacious room. "The apartment I found doesn't allow animals."

Royce swayed, touching the top of his desk to steady himself. She'd actually done it, actually located an apartment. She was going to leave him.

A pain knifed through the core of him, so sharp and hot it took his breath away.

Fidgeting with her fingers, Laura slipped a glance at

Maggie, who yawned and blinked, seemingly unconcerned that her own feline world was in jeopardy. "Wendy will take Sam, the Wyncrofts' son and daughter-in-law are interested in Bunny-Cat, and the Hendersons have agreed to adopt Patches. I'm still hoping to find homes for Rascal and Cary Grant, but I don't know what I'll do about Maggie." She covered a break in her voice with a strained cough and balled her hands together in a tight knot. "It's difficult to place an adult cat, particularly one who is, ah, somewhat temperamental."

Royce wanted to sweep Laura into his arms and kiss her senseless. Instead, he willed his legs into motion and sat in a guest chair a few feet from the settee. "Maggie can stay here."

A rush of tears brightened her eyes. "Thank you," she whispered. "Once again I find myself grateful for your generosity."

Swallowing a lump in his throat, Royce cooled his face with his hands. "I'm the one who is grateful, Laura. You and Jamie have brought joy and laughter into my life. I—" He struggled for words.

What could he tell her? That he laid awake nights aching to hold her, that the fragrance from her steamy showers wafted into his lungs like liquid fire until he was insane with wanting her, needing her? Could he confess that she had invaded his thoughts, his dreams, every fiber of his being?

"I'll miss you," he said finally.

Her flinch was so subtle that he might have missed it had his greedy gaze not been riveted on every nuance of her expression. "We'll miss you, too."

He sucked a breath, expelled it, drew in another. He leaned forward in the chair, his elbows crooked and his fingers twitching with a desperate need to stroke her soft hair, caress her silken cheek, to simply touch her one last time.

"Laura—"

"Royce—"

Startled that they'd blurted each other's name at the same moment, both fell silent, smiling self-consciously.

"You first," Royce said.

Laura shifted, chewed her lip. The adorable dimple beside her mouth deepened as if daring him to lean forward and nuzzle it. "I wanted to apologize."

"For what?"

"For criticizing your business decisions. I know how much the company means to you. You have a right and a responsibility to do whatever is necessary to save it."

Slowly, Royce leaned back in the chair. He propped his ankle on his knee and shifted sideways to drape his arm over the backrest. It was a position of relaxed authority he used automatically whenever he felt threatened or guilty. "I do have a responsibility, Laura, to the hundreds of people whose jobs I can save if I make the right decision."

"I know that." Flushing, she looked away. "I was speaking from my heart, not my head. It's just that—" She paused a beat, then issued a sigh. "Never mind."

"Tell me. Please."

She shrugged. "It's just that I keep thinking there must be another way."

"I'll entertain any suggestions you care to offer."

Apparently that was the opening she'd been seeking. Although she was looking away from him, her eyes rolled to the side, angling a glance in his direction. "I'm sure this is a silly idea, but..." A sparkle of triumph in her eyes put him on guard. "What exactly is profit-sharing?"

He blinked. "It's a process where employees of a company earn bonuses above their wage structure based on meeting or exceeding certain production or profit criteria."

"In other words, an incentive to work harder and produce more, because the more profit the company earns, the higher the employee bonus?"

"Basically."

"And what are stock options?"

He narrowed his gaze, certain she already had all the answers to the questions she was now posing. "Again, there are various ways of structuring stock options, but most involve allowing employees to contribute financially to the company in return for certain equity."

She widened her eyes as if that was amazing news. "Really? My, that sounds as if it could be a wonderful incentive. Instead of merely working for a company, employees actually become partial owners, accepting the risks and reaping the rewards of their investment."

Folding his arms, he regarded her, not fooled by her innocent stare. Laura was a highly intelligent woman, and if his assessment of this bizarre conversation was accurate, she was also a brilliant tactician. "*Risk* is the definitive word, Laura. Expanding the base of decision-makers dilutes organizational control."

"In other words, you would personally lose power."

He blinked. "Yes."

To her credit, she maintained an impassive expression. "Then I can see why you'd be hesitant to embrace such a radical idea." She stood, smoothing the front of her crisp white blouse, which drew attention to the sleek skirt hugging her curvaceous hips like a second skin. "I told you it was a silly idea."

He stood, frowning. "Are you implying that personal power is more important to me than the well-being of my employees?"

She met his gaze directly. "Is it?"

Denial teetered on his tongue but stubbornly refused to announce itself. "You don't have a very high opinion of me, do you, Laura?"

Her gaze softened. "You are a fine and decent man, Royce, a man who has overcome immense challenge to rise to the pinnacle of your profession. You've provided outstanding products to millions of grateful consumers, and excellent jobs to thousands of thriving employees. Through it all, your priorities have never wavered. That's why you've been so successful in the past, and will continue to be successful in the future."

When she turned to leave, he touched her shoulder, stopping her. His hand lingered a moment, slipping down her arm before he reluctantly released her. "Just what are my priorities, Laura?"

For a moment, he thought she might answer, but at the last moment she sighed and looked away. "If you don't know, I certainly can't tell you. The answer is in your own heart, Royce. Look there, and you'll find what you are seeking."

Their eyes met for a moment, a moment of bliss and despair, of aching desire tempered with stinging loss. Then she stepped away and left the room.

Trembling, Royce lowered himself back into the guest chair, propped his elbows on his thighs and bent forward, breathing hard. He fought a wave of nausea at the realization that she was truly going to leave him. He'd driven her away, deliberately, methodically, with the cool cruelty of a man so terrified by the power of his own emotions that he was willing to destroy anyone who ventured close enough to jeopardize that coveted self-control.

Footsteps jarred him upright. He touched his burning eyelids a moment before Marta entered the room. "What is it?" he snapped.

Marta jerked to a stop, obviously stunned by his tone.

Groaning, he stood, spun away from the chair and paced the room, clasping his hands behind his back. When he'd regained his composure, he took a deep breath. "Forgive me, Marta. My foul mood is not your fault." His gaze fell on a small velvet box nested in her palms. "What is that?"

The woman studied the box as if she'd never seen it before. "It just came for Mrs. Burton. By courier." She licked her lips and met Royce's quizzical gaze. "Yes, I opened it. I wanted to see what kind of extravagant bauble she thought herself worth."

It took a moment for the impact to sink in. "You had no right to violate Laura's privacy in that manner."

"I know."

"You will return the item to her immediately, with your apologies."

Slowly, Marta shook her head. "No, I don't think so."

"What?" Royce vibrated as if shaken by giant hands. "Are you refusing to obey my instructions?"

"Yes, I suppose I am." A sheen of tears brightened her blue eyes, leaked onto her lined cheek. She held the tiny box out to him. "This doesn't belong to Laura. It belongs to you."

After a moment's hesitation, he accepted the velvet container, planning to return it to Laura immediately.

"Open it," Marta urged. "Please."

For some strange reason, Royce's hands performed the function even as his mind insisted otherwise. His traitorous fingers lifted the small lid, which snapped up to reveal the golden contents. He heard a stunned gasp, knew that the sound had come from him.

Images from the past flew through his mind, the flash of his laughing mother painting at her easel, the memory of Laura sneaking out of his study with a camera in her hand. He spun to stare at the watercolors on the wall, focusing on his mother's trademark signature.

"My God," he murmured. He glanced from the paintings to Marta, who was sobbing openly, then back into the open jewelry box, where a pair of golden cuff links blinked up at him. Each cuff link was etched with his mother's initials, and a four-leaf clover wrapped in ivy.

"It's a gift," Marta whispered between sobs. "She knew how much it would mean to you."

"Yes," he murmured. "She knew."

Touched beyond measure, Royce moved to his desk and dropped into his swivel chair. His placed the box on his desk, his gaze never wavering from the cherished contents. Without conscious thought, he opened the desk drawer, extracted the small wooden box in which he'd kept the seashell Sabrina had given him so many years ago.

Sabrina had never loved him. And truth be told, he had never loved her. He had simply needed her memory as a shield to protect himself, protect his emotions. Protect his priorities.

Laura had been right about him. Royce had always

kept his eye on his priorities: success, power, control. The human factor was never included, beyond routine kindness that could be bestowed without jeopardizing what was truly important to him.

That was what he remembered when he'd held Sabrina's seashell in his palm, not the love he'd felt but the reminder of one whose priorities mirrored his own.

He handed the shell box to Marta. "Dispose of this. I won't be needing it anymore."

She nodded, took a step toward the door, then paused to look over her shoulder. "Laura is a good woman. You could do worse."

No reply was expected, and none was given.

Royce continued to stare at the lovely cuff links long after Marta had left the room. He marveled at the intricacy, tracing the miniature etching with his fingertips. The image was so finely drawn that every glance refreshed the image of his beloved mother, smiling and vibrant, doing what she loved.

Somehow Laura had known that, had understood that was the memory Royce needed, the reminder that Joyce Leeds Burton was a woman who had found joy and contentment amid the drudgery and poverty of life. Laura had peered deeply into Royce's soul, extracted one spark of happiness in the bleakness of past despair, and had molded that tiny flame into a flaring beacon of hope for the future.

His mother's priority had always been love, love of her child, of beauty and joy, of friendship and devotion. That had been her legacy to him, a legacy Royce had forgotten in his quest for respect from those who had once shunned him. Somewhere along the way, he'd lost sight of the path so lovingly laid out for him. With Laura's help, he'd found it again.

Without taking his eyes off the gleaming golden gift, he lifted the telephone receiver and dialed.

"I can't believe you're moving to Alaska." Stunned, Laura dropped into the worn sofa, barely noticing the vibration of the mobile home as two exuberant boys dashed out the front door. "Daniel lives in a barracks with a dozen other men. You can't just barge in there with two young children."

Smiling, Wendy finished drying a plastic glass, gazed across the breakfast counter with a serenity Laura had never seen in the harried mom. "We'll find a cabin or pitch a tent or something."

"Pitch a tent? It drops to seventy below zero on the tundra."

She laughed. "Okay, a tent with a wood stove. The family will finally be together again. That's all that really matters."

"This isn't funny, Wendy. It's not like you to be so impulsive, especially when it comes to your children's security."

Laying down the dishcloth, Wendy poured two glasses of iced tea and carried them into the tiny living room. She handed one to Laura, then placed her own glass on the coffee table. "I understand what you're saying, Laura. God knows that up until last night, I even agreed with you."

"What happened last night?"

"Daniel called." Her eyes lit like glowing candles. "We talked for hours, Laura, really talked. It occurred to both of us that in our zeal to give our kids all the security and luxuries we thought they needed, we were depriving them of the one thing that was most important to them. The nurturing support of a loving family.''

Cradling the icy glass between her palms, Laura studied her friend's relaxed smile, but was still unconvinced that such a momentous decision had been rationally arrived at. ''Sometimes short-term sacrifice has to be made for the long-term good.''

She flinched at the realization that her statement bore startling similarity to something Royce had once said.

Clearing her throat, Laura made a lame attempt to clarify. ''I mean, you and Daniel had mapped out your financial future, made plans that would ensure your children all the educational opportunities they needed to secure a place in the world. Now, after all the hardships, you're willing to give all that up?''

''We're not giving up our dreams,'' Wendy said. ''We've simply decided that the price we've been paying is too high.''

Plucking the glass out of Laura's grasp, Wendy set it aside and cupped her friend's hand between her own warm palms.

''You know what Timmy did the other day?'' Sorrow flashed through Wendy's eyes at the memory. ''He asked to see pictures of Daddy, so he could remember what he looked like. Can you imagine that, Laura? We have been so intent on providing our children with what they'll need in the future that we have lost sight of what they need right now.''

A fission of truth skimmed down Laura's spine. She knew that Wendy was right. Deep in her soul, she knew it; she just couldn't quite accept it, because to do so would lead in the direction that her own wounded heart yearned to travel. ''But just yesterday you were so frightened about all that you stood to lose.''

"That's because I wasn't looking at all that we stood to gain." Inhaling deeply, Wendy glanced around the tiny cluttered home with a poignant smile. "This place has been good to us. It has sheltered us, kept us warm, given us a sense of belonging. But it was never truly a home, because it also kept us from being a family. Things don't really matter, Laura, people matter. Memories matter, because life is finite. When it's over, all we have left of those we cherished is the memory of what they have shared with us. I want my boys to have those memories. I want them to know that we love them more than we love comfort or security or material possessions. I want us to be a family again."

"No matter what it takes?"

"No matter what."

Laura blinked away a burn of tears. "I'll miss you so much," she whispered.

"I'll miss you, too." Wendy's eyes brightened with moisture. "I hope you understand why we have to do this."

"I do understand," Laura replied, surprised to realize that it was true. "In fact, I envy you for having figured out what is truly important in life before it was too late."

Wendy tilted her head, regarded her thoughtfully. "Happiness has already knocked, Laura. It's not too late to open the door, and let it into your life."

Chapter Fourteen

Laura studied the sleek black gown draped on its satin-padded hanger, and the sequined royal-blue cocktail dress hanging beside it. She contemplated leaving the items behind, along with the bittersweet memories they evoked. They didn't actually belong to her, at least not yet. She'd made only a few payments on the garments, and she still owed more than she could comfortably afford.

And she was in debt up to her eyebrows to the local jewelry boutique for the cuff links she'd ordered for Royce. It occurred to her that she had yet to see the items, which should have been delivered earlier in the week. She made a mental note to call the shop, then carefully arranged the plastic garment protectors over the designer gowns and replaced them in the closet, wishing she hadn't committed herself to absorb the cost of such extravagant clothing.

Gathering an armful of items from her dresser, she loaded the open suitcase on the bed until it bulged from the strain. The remainder of her clothing would have to be boxed, she supposed, although it didn't matter much. It was only a fifteen-minute drive to the small apartment she'd located on the far side of town. The place was rather drab, not terribly roomy, but it was close to Jamie's day-care center and the elementary school he'd be attending in a few years.

As she folded her remaining garments into neat piles on the luxurious bed, the sound of a vehicle caught her attention. A glance out the window confirmed that Royce had returned home. Since it wasn't unusual for him to return to the house throughout the day, she wasn't surprised by his appearance.

Still, her heart rate spiked at the sight of him as he stepped from the sleek sedan, handsome as always in a tailored business suit. He strode to the porch purposefully, with the lengthy step of a man on a mission. She smiled, swallowing a lump in her throat.

Why was it, she wondered, that she always fell in love with men who were unwilling or unable to return that coveted emotion?

And she did love Royce Burton, deeply, profoundly, with every fiber of her being.

That was, of course, her problem, not his.

Sighing, she returned to her packing, deliberately focusing on the chore with enough determination that she didn't hear footsteps in the upstairs hall until a moment before her bedroom door swung open.

Gasping, she spun around, clutching her chest. "Don't you believe in knocking?"

Royce regarded her impassively. "I didn't mean to startle you."

"Well, you did." Breathing hard, she turned away and absently fiddled with a stack of folded sweaters. "As long as you're here, could you make yourself useful and take that suitcase downstairs, where the other boxes are stacked? The movers will be here any minute."

"Actually, they won't. I took the liberty of canceling your appointment with them."

"You did what?" Squaring her shoulders, she straightened slowly, faced him with wary disbelief. "May I presume that you did so because you wish to lug our belongings across town with your two hands? Because that's about the only acceptable excuse I can think of for such presumptuous behavior."

"There's another excuse, one I hope you'll also find reasonable under the circumstance."

"And that would be...?"

He shifted his stance, gave his collar an endearingly nervous tug, then stepped forward to offer what appeared to be a thin, bound report. "I wanted you to have sufficient opportunity to review this before you, ah, made a final decision about leaving."

Something in his eyes gave her pause. She moistened her lips and dried her palms on her jeans. "I've already made a final decision, Royce. Your lawyer is preparing marriage dissolution papers as we speak."

A crimson flush brightened his jaw. "Actually, he's not."

She narrowed her gaze. "Let me guess...you've taken the liberty of canceling the legal paperwork as well."

"Merely postponing it," he mumbled. "I'd hoped you wouldn't mind."

"I do mind."

"Yes, I can see that you do." He cleared his throat, laid the report atop a stack of folded clothing on the bed. "Perhaps after you've reviewed these figures, you'll feel differently."

"I don't want to review anything," she said, although her reluctant gaze traveled to the cover sheet of the report he'd laid on the bed. "I need to finish this packing before Jamie wakes up from his nap, then I have to see the landlord about signing the lease, then I must have the utilities turned on—"

Royce interrupted by snatching up the report and placing directly in her hand. "Just read it. Please."

Her fingers convulsed, clutching the bound document as if it were a lifeline. "All right."

Relief flooded his gaze. He issued a nervous smile, clasping his hands behind his back as she seated herself on an uncluttered edge of the mattress.

She read the title page aloud. "Capital Enhancement Alternatives, A Comparative Study." Frowning, she glanced up. "What does that mean?"

A nervous pucker pulled at his brows. He gestured with his hand, giving a curt nod indicating that she should continue reading. She shrugged, and did so.

By the end of the first page, Laura understood exactly what the report was proposing. By the end of the final page, she understood how dear the cost of that proposal would be. For Royce, and for her.

She looked up, shaken and speechless.

Royce sucked a deep breath, exhaled all at once. "You see, you were right. There was another option."

Laura found her voice. "A dangerous one."

"Yes, there's considerable risk."

That was an understatement. The crux of the report was a revised fiscal forecast based on the presumption

that Burton Technologies had refused Marchandt's offer of capital, opting instead to give the workers themselves the opportunity to invest in their own company
by buying stock, lowering their own salaries in return
for future profit-sharing incentives.

There was a downside to the idea, however, and it
was a big one. Although the plan had long-range potential, it couldn't raise enough initial capital for immediate expansion, which could result in financial disaster.

"You realize," Royce said, "that the first years of
implementation would be crucial to either the success
or failure of the plan. There are no guarantees here.
Bankruptcy is a very real threat. The company may not
survive."

She was sick with fear. The company meant everything to Royce. Its loss would devastate him. "Are you
willing to risk that?"

"Are you?" His gaze deepened, held her in place
with mesmerizing intensity. "If the company folds, I
won't have the resources to fulfill my end of our bargain. There won't be enough money to maintain this
house, to keep up appearances in society circles, to give
you the financial security you need and deserve. I may
not even be able to afford the legal expenses necessary
to keep your ex in-laws at bay."

Her fingers automatically flexed with fear, not for
herself but for Royce. Tears leaked into her eyes, tears
for a man courageous enough and generous enough to
risk everything dear to him for the sake of others. "I
understand that."

"Do you? Do you really understand?" He dropped
to one knee beside the bed and took her hand. "I
wouldn't be able to offer you any of the things you

deserve, Laura. Life would be a struggle. Even if the company survived, it would be years before my personal assets would compare with what I have now. If the worst happened, we'd be finally destitute, and all those jobs we tried to save would be gone, anyway.''

That he'd repeatedly used the pronoun ''we'' did not escape her notice. Before she could gather her thoughts to comment on that, a golden glimmer at his wrists caught her eye. ''The cuff links. Where did you get them?''

''They were a gift,'' he murmured, kissing her fingertips. ''From someone I love very much.''

Her heart leapt as if seeking escape. Without knowing what she would say, she parted her lips to respond.

''Wait.'' Royce silenced her by tenderly touching her mouth with the tip of his finger. ''Let me say this before I lose my nerve.''

Any words she wished to utter were already clogged behind the lump of emotion in her throat, so she merely widened her eyes and nodded.

Royce licked his lips. ''I have never been in love before,'' he said finally. ''I thought I was once…twice, if my second-grade teacher, who broke my heart by marrying an investment banker before I was old enough to woo her myself, counts.''

Not knowing what to say, Laura said nothing. She was riveted to the vulnerability she saw in Royce's eyes, and knew that he was about to express something momentous. Something that would change both of their lives forever.

''Over the years, I steeled myself against matters of the heart by telling myself that love was a selfish emotion, built more on what one reaps from the relationship rather than what is sown.'' Royce paused for breath.

When he spoke again, his voice broke. "You changed all that for me, Laura, you and Jamie. You brought true joy into my world, a deeper meaning to my existence. I can accept a life without personal wealth and privilege. I can accept a life where my own power is again sublimated to that of others. These things I can live with. I cannot, however, imagine a life without you and Jamie being a part of it."

Laura's breath came in shallow puffs. Her mind was spinning, her heart ready to burst. "That is the sweetest, most precious thing anyone has ever said to me."

His gaze searched hers. "I have no right to ask you to stay, but I'll ask it, anyway. I want you to be my wife, Laura, my lawfully wedded wife from this day forward. I want to be a real husband to you, a real father to Jamie and to all the other children that I pray we will someday share. I know it's selfish, Laura, asking you to risk everything for a man as flawed and arrogant as I—"

Now it was Laura's turn to silence him by laying a gentle finger to his lips. "You are not a selfish man, Royce Burton. You are the kindest, dearest and most generous person I have ever met. I would follow you into a castle or the poorhouse, and consider myself blessed simply to stand by your side. It doesn't matter to me where we live, or how we live. I don't care if—" she smiled at the memory of Wendy's glowing gaze "—if you pitch a tent on the Alaskan tundra, as long as we live there together as a real family."

He blinked. "It's quite cold in Alaska, isn't it?"

"We'll buy a wood stove." She laughed, framing his face with her palms. "I love you with all my heart, Royce. I've loved you from the moment I first laid eyes on you, and I will continue to love you until I take my final breath on this earth.''

He turned his face just enough to press a kiss against her palm, then angled a sexy smile. "Is that a 'yes,' Mrs. Burton?"

"That is most definitely a 'yes,' Mr. Burton."

"Excellent." He stood, urging her upward with a gentle tug on her hand. "Jamie should sleep for another hour or so, shouldn't he?"

"I suppose so, but—" She let out a gasp as he lifted her into his arms and carried her into the hallway. "Where are we going?"

"Into our bedroom, wife. I have some husbandly duties to perform." A thin meow captured his attention. He gazed down at the orange cat at his feet. "No, you may not watch."

Seeming perplexed by the peculiar privacy required for human mating rituals, Maggie twitched her tail, then rotated her shoulders in the feline equivalent of a shrug, as if making allowances for the odd behavior of a species less evolved than her own.

Laura chuckled as Royce carried her into the master suite. "Husbandly duties," she murmured. "I like the sound of that."

"So do I." He closed the door with an artful kick. "Let the honeymoon begin."

Epilogue

"Daddy's home, Daddy's home!" Flinging out his fat arms, Jamie hurled himself forward before Royce could take two steps inside the front door. "Pick me up, Daddy, pick me *way* up!"

"Hey, champ." Royce dropped his briefcase on the floor, lifted the giggling youngster up and sat him on his shoulders. "How's my big boy today?"

"Rascal ate a grasshopper!"

"He did?"

"Uh-huh. Him showed it to Auntie Marta, and she screamed really loud, so him ate it."

"Well, ah, good for Rascal. I think." Royce grimaced, sidled a glance at Laura, who'd just entered the room smiling and rubbing the small of her back. "I don't suppose this is a good time to ask what Marta's fixing for dinner."

"Fear not," she said with a laugh. "Rascal escaped Marta's wrath. He's hunkered under Jamie's bed, sulking." She paused to pet the ever-sleek and sophisticated Cary Grant, who was sprawled across the back of the sofa, then moved through the diminutive foyer and tipped her head. "Kiss me, husband."

"With pleasure, wife." He obliged, cherishing her sweetness as if it were the first time he'd tasted it.

Royce had heard that the thrill of romantic love lessened over time, that marriage quickly turned into a dull routine. So far that hadn't happened. After more than a year of wedded bliss, every touch of his true love's lips was more exciting than the last, and the radiance of her smile lit a bonfire of gratitude deep inside him.

She and Jamie were everything to him. Royce couldn't even remember what his life had been like before they were a part of it.

"Bounce me, Daddy, bounce me!" Jamie squirmed on Royce's shoulder, bopping him lightly on the head to get his attention. "I want a horsey ride."

Laura shifted in his embrace, reaching up to still the child's hands. "Give your father a moment to relax, sweetums. Maybe then he'll give you a horsey ride."

Royce felt the dejected slump of the youngster's little body, and was stung by it. "That's okay, honey, I don't mind giving him a quick gallop."

"I mind. I'm selfish. For the next five minutes, I want all of your attention, and I want it all to myself."

When she reached up as if to lift the wriggling three-year-old down, Royce stopped her. Stepping aside, he swung Jamie gently to the floor and gathered his wife in his arms as the exuberant youngster dashed out of the room. "You know the doctor told you not to lift anything heavy."

Her light laugh was music to his ears. "I'm pregnant, not disabled."

"I know." He caressed her swollen belly, bent to kiss it while she stroked his hair. "I worry, that's all."

"There's nothing to worry about," she murmured. "Our daughter is just fine, and in about five weeks you'll be able to see that for yourself."

"I can hardly wait."

"Neither can I."

She hugged him fiercely, nested her head beneath his chin. "There you are," she murmured as Maggie meandered into the room. "And where were you when your troublemaking child was terrorizing poor Marta?"

The mama cat blinked, yawned hugely and leapt onto her favorite napping spot. The burgundy chair now occupied a spot in the living room since Royce's new study was considerably smaller than the old one had been.

"I guess she figures now that her babies have grown up, they're on their own," Royce said. "There's barely enough room for the humans in this place, let alone three cats."

"There's plenty of room. Besides, you know you love them."

Royce grumbled under his breath, a feigned annoyance that served more to amuse Laura than concern her. She frequently teased him about his terrible flaw of detesting felines, and usually chose a moment when he'd been caught in the act of affectionate nuzzling with one of the furry terrors. "Those cats act as if they own the place."

"In their mind they do." Laura shifted, stroked his chin with her fingertip. "By the way, we'll have to use the hall shower for a few days. Ours is clogged again."

A jitter of guilt quickened his pulse. He swore under his breath.

She glanced up, regarding him with that sage expression that always made him feel as if she could see right through him. "It's all right, Royce."

"No, it isn't all right. You're entitled to a shower that works when you want it to work without having to call a plumber every two weeks."

Even though the company's profit-sharing expansion plan had been Laura's idea, Royce felt guilty about the lifestyle changes required to accommodate the venture. Deep down, there was still a niggling need to lavish those he loved with material things and damn the cost.

Laura understood that about him, and offered constant reassurance that she didn't need extravagance to be happy. Family was all that counts, she'd once told him. As long as the family was together, nothing else mattered.

Royce knew that she had meant that, meant it with all her heart. Laura loved him nearly as much as he loved her, and would continue to love him whether he was a pauper or a king. Of course, he was far from destitute. On paper he was still worth a fortune, although most of his liquid assets had been churned back into the company.

Laura seemed to read his mind. "I love this house, Royce. It's comfortable and homey, and I don't need a map to find my way around in it."

"It's a little crowded."

"It's got four bedrooms, three bathrooms, a study

and private quarters for Marta," she pointed out. "It is hardly a hovel."

"I just want the best for you."

"I have the best," she whispered. "I have you."

* * * * *

*Look for Catrina Mitchell Jordan's story
in the next book of Diana Whitney's*
STORK EXPRESS *series,*

MIXING BUSINESS...WITH BABY

*in Silhouette Romance (#1490)
in late December.*

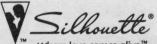

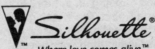

#1 *New York Times* bestselling author

NORA ROBERTS

introduces the loyal and loving, tempestuous and tantalizing Stanislaski family.

Coming in November 2000:

The Stanislaski Brothers
Mikhail and Alex

Their immigrant roots and warm, supportive home had made Mikhail and Alex Stanislaski both strong and passionate. And their charm makes them irresistible....

In February 2001, watch for
THE STANISLASKI SISTERS: *Natasha and Rachel*

And a brand-new Stanislaski story from Silhouette Special Edition,
CONSIDERING KATE

Available at your favorite retail outlet.

Silhouette®
Where love comes alive™